PAGES, PAWPRINTS, AND POISON

A charity bake, a banned book, and a teacup with teeth

Copyright © 2025 by Ivy Grant

Cover designed by Azameti Michael

Published by Azameti Michael

All rights reserved. No part of this book may be reproduced, distributed, or transmitted in any form or by any means, electronic or mechanical, including photocopying, recording, or any information storage and retrieval system, without the prior written permission of the publisher, except in the case of brief quotations embodied in critical reviews and certain other non-commercial uses permitted by copyright law.

This is a work of fiction. Names, characters, places, and incidents are either the product of the author's imagination or used fictitiously. Any resemblance to actual persons, living or dead, or actual events is purely coincidental. For information about this title or to request permission for use, please contact:

greyama70@gmail.com

First Edition, 2025

BOOK TWO

PEPPERMINT CAT BOOKSHOP MYSTERIES

TABLE OF CONTENTS

Chapter 1: Display Day
Chapter 2: Bake Tent Bustle
Chapter 3: Cup Confusion
Chapter 4: Ballot Batch
Chapter 5: PTA Smoke
Chapter 6: Flour Trail
Chapter 7: Pen Match
Chapter 8: Promo Grudge
Chapter 9: Pastry Alibi
Chapter 10: Teacup Glaze
Chapter 11: Shelf Sit
Chapter 12: Claim Ticket
Chapter 13: Residue Test
Chapter 14: Ledger Audit
Chapter 15: Donor Past
Chapter 16: Spouse Pressure
Chapter 17: Confrontation
Chapter 18: Arrest
Chapter 19: Community Reset
Chapter 20: Cat and Cups
ABOUT THE AUTHOR

CHAPTER 1

Display Day

Morning slipped into Peppermint Cat like it understood the assignment. The front windows took a pale shine. The bell gave one clear note. I set the banned-and-challenged table where the light would catch the cover art without bleaching it. No drama, only context. Each book got a small placard with a short quote about why it had been challenged, and a second line about why it still matters. I keep the language tight. People read the whole card when you cut the fat.

Peppermint leaped onto the table and sat square in front of a paperback with a stack of paper cranes on the cover. He tucked his paws under and blinked the slow blink of a cat who has chosen a hill to die on. I lifted him and set him on the poetry shelf. He hopped back to the banned table and planted himself between a memoir and a picture book about colors. So the censor in fur was on duty. Fine. He could guard the display while I set the bake tent.

Rafi wheeled a rack of folding tables to the alley. He moves like a man who has measured the world and found it slightly too wide, so he trims it with lists. He parked the rack, checked the time, and held up the donation ledger for my initials. We keep a clean chain on fundraiser days. Every dollar in, every dollar out, no smears. His first line of the day sat neat in blue ballpoint with his slight rightward lean. "Community Literacy Fund, opening balance," then the zero, then the time. No one could move that entry with a story later. Rafi writes like a witness.

"Placards are crisp," he said.

"Short and fair," I said. "If Nina starts a scene, the cards will do the talking until Asa finishes his coffee."

Rafi smiled into his mug. "The kettle knows when you jinx it."

The shop smelled like cinnamon and printer ink. I carried the last placard to the front. A small crowd had begun to form on the sidewalk. Bake sales do that. Add a table full of banned titles and you collect the curious with their coins already in their hands.

Harold Keene came in with his steady stride and a blazer he should have retired last fall. He is the kind of donor who reads the receipts. He stopped at the table, took in the spread, and nodded like he was counting fence posts.

"This looks honest," he said. "Not a shout. A case."

"That's the point," I said.

He turned to the growing audience and raised his voice one notch. "I'm matching the first five hundred for the literacy fund," he said. "Keep your receipts." He tapped the ledger with one finger. "And keep this neat. The county likes its books balanced."

The county also likes its donors steady. Harold had been steady for years. That is why the day would take a turn people would remember for the wrong reason.

Nina Carrow arrived with a camera-ready scowl and a tote that wanted to be a podium. PTA hair sprayed to behave, cardigan in the same school colors she loves to weaponize, little gold charm shaped like an apple at her throat. She took three photos of the table, one of Peppermint, none of the placards. She inhaled like a person about to launch a speech and caught me watching.

"Children walk in this store," she said. "They do not need to see filth on a front table."

"They see a reading list," I said. "With context. If a parent wants to talk, I have tea and chairs."

She huffed and snapped a close-up of a title she has never read. "I will bring this to the board."

"You bring everything to the board," I said. "Bring your receipts. We have ours."

Her eyes flicked to the ledger in Rafi's hands and then to the crowd. Parents. Teens. A pair of retirees who play cribbage at the bakery on Thursdays. The town was here for a bake sale and a book table, not a speech. She swallowed the rest of her sentence and stepped back to muster allies on the sidewalk thread.

Bria Leduc crossed from the alley with a box balanced on one forearm and a grin built for cameras. She had done three pop-up stalls this summer and won two blue ribbons at the fair. People like her lemon bars. She likes them liking her lemon bars. She set out rows in perfect geometry and placed a card with neat loops. "Bria's Citrus Bars." She asked me to check the spacing as if the world might end if a bar sat a quarter inch off the line. Rafi gave her a thumbs-up. I gave her a pot of peppermint tea for the tent table. She wrinkled her nose at the steam. She drinks coffee like a dockhand.

Paula Hines slipped in behind a stack of donated hardcovers. Librarian bag, comfort shoes, a calm that looks like quiet until she talks and you realize she knows the room better than you do. She ran a finger along a placard and smiled without showing teeth. "You kept the quotes tight," she said. "They read like a spine."

"I stole a line from you," I said.

"That's fair," she said. "I steal mugs from you."

Behind her, Martin Keene eased through the door. Harold's husband dresses like a committee meeting. The right shirt. The right belt. The wrong smile if you know what to look for. He scanned the table, then the ledger, then the faces. He claimed a corner by the espresso bar and began to text like a man building a shield out of time stamps.

"Your donor is on message," he said to the room, loud enough that people could hear his support. "We love literacy. We love decency too."

"Good," I said. "We have room for both."

Rafi set an overflow tray by the espresso bar for cups that would need a place to land. The tent had its own matched set of white cups and saucers in a crate near the back door. The shop keeps a motley crew of thrift-store survivors. Today I had pulled six from the cupboard in case we ran hot at the bar. Five matched in a plain, glossy set. One did not. I noticed it when I set the tray. The glaze on that odd cup showed a fine starburst of crazing that looked like frost on glass. Old. Pretty if you like that sort of thing. The handle had a hairline crack that had darkened over years of tea. The saucer for that one was missing. I made a note to keep it near the sink and not in circulation.

Peppermint left the banned table and jumped onto the counter. He planted his tail against the overflow tray. His whiskers brushed the odd cup. He blinked and turned away. Peppermint is not a forensic tech. He is a cat who thinks cups are small thrones. Still, I moved the odd one two inches back from his reach.

Outside, the tent took shape. Two high schoolers strung bunting. Rafi taped the donation jar to the center table. The church sent over a sheet for the windward side. The alley light slanted across flour dust like confetti. It looked like a day written to go well.

"Time," Rafi said, tapping his watch.

I rang the bell and the crowd shifted into lines. Coins clinked. The Square reader chirped. Paula chatted with a grandmother about a read-aloud program. Nina performed indignation in a three-foot radius that did not disturb anyone with a fork already in hand. Bria handed out bars with the confidence of a person who knows her layer ratios.

Harold moved from table to table like a grandparent at a picnic. He held a small plate of something that looked like pecan. He tilted it toward strangers like an invitation. People spoke to him. People like to speak to donors. He stopped by Bria's table and put a lemon bar on his plate. He stopped at the tea urn and poured. He brought the cup to his face and inhaled with a small flash of pride. He likes to say he can tell peppermint and spearmint apart with his eyes closed. He turned toward the door of the shop for a better photo in the light. Several phones lifted. He lifted his cup for the camera. It was a good shot. The angle, the donor, the words on the banned sign behind his shoulder. I watched him like you watch a person you are responsible for because you run the room where he is standing.

He took a sip. He smiled. It was the smile people wear when they confirm a memory with their mouth. He took another.

There is a tiny sound a teacup makes when a hand lets it slip. Not the hard clink of a plate on tile. A soft surrender. The sound came first. Harold's fingers lost their place around the handle. The cup kissed the pavement and rolled. He blinked as if surprised to find his legs attached to the ground. His knees gave, then his shoulder, then his cheek. He went down in a slow collapse that made time run in stripes.

I called the time out loud. "Twelve fourteen." People make better witnesses when you give them a number to tie their breath to. I told Bria to step back. I told Rafi to call Asa Quinn. I told the high schoolers to lift the bunting and give us a pocket of air. Paula took one look and moved to the far table to keep the children busy. She started a game that looked like an inventory of sprinkles. She is fast when the room needs a hand.

I knelt by Harold and looked at his face. No gore. No dramatic pallor. A soft sheen on his upper lip. A tremor along the jaw. I did not touch the cup. I saw where it had rolled. It sat on its side under the edge of the table leg. The glaze caught the light. A fine map of starburst lines. The odd cup from the overflow tray, not the tent set. My notes made a small click in my head. Things talk when you let them.

"Rafi," I said. "Mark the cup."

"Already on it," he said. He laid down a small ring of pastry string from his apron and lifted his phone for three quick shots. He writes with a lean. He photographs like that too. Real, efficient, clean.

A circle formed and then held at the edge. People want to step in. They also want to be told to stop. I stood and faced the crowd and kept my voice steady.

"We have an emergency," I said. "Deputy Quinn is on the way. Please step back three paces and keep the aisle to the door clear."

They did it. You can move a crowd if you sound like a person who knows where they are going.

Nina moved in the opposite direction of my instruction because of course she did. She put her hand to her throat and delivered indignation to a phone held by Sylvie Tran, who runs a local feed that eats conflict like cookies. Nina's hair did not move even though the wind had decided to live in the alley. She angling her body to make sure the banned table sat behind her shoulder in the frame.

"This is what happens when a shop promotes obscenity," she said. "The mood is poisoned. The community is hurt. This is what we warned you about."

Sylvie nodded at the cadence and did not commit on substance. She only needs a clip. Context is for later.

"Paula," I said without looking away from the ground. "The ledger."

She already had it. She had the sense to hold it inside the shop, on the counter, next to the register, under the camera. Her librarian brain and my shop brain track in the same direction most days.

Rafi leaned into my line of sight. "Asa is three minutes," he said. "He was two blocks away at the clinic."

"Good," I said. "Keep people comfortable."

He lifted the kettle. He knows how to pour steadiness into paper cups.

Harold's husband had moved closer. Martin stood inside the shop, framed by the espresso bar, phone in his hand, face composed into sympathy for the waiting audience. I saw his eyes track the odd cup on the ground, then cut to the overflow tray, then back to the cup. He had counted the cups too.

I bent, put on gloves, and reached under the table with a cloth to draw the cup toward me without smearing the dust on the sidewalk. I did not lift it. I took a closer look in the angle where the chalky glaze met the curve. Crazing lines. The thin hairline at the handle foot. The faint tea tide line inside, slightly higher than the marks in the tent cups I had unpacked this morning. Not proof, just the first rung of a ladder you climb later when the room is calm and the gloves change.

Asa stepped into the alley with his coat unbuttoned and his pen ready. He reads the room first. Then he speaks.

"Time," he said.

"Twelve fourteen," I said.

He moved to Harold with a medic's caution and an investigator's economy. He checked pulse, breath, eyes. He did not perform medicine he does not have. He marked what he saw. He asked for the cup and I pointed, hand still.

"I can bag it," he said.

"I would like a photo of it in place without shadow," I said. "Then yes."

He gave me the look we reserve for people who make our jobs easier, then took his shots and slid the cup into a clear sleeve with the rim facing up. He sealed the bag and wrote the time on the strip. He set it on the table as if it were a small animal that needed air.

"Anyone drink from this before Harold," he asked the ring.

Silence finds the edges of a crowd slowly. Bria raised her hand. "I set out tent cups only," she said. "No shop cups came outside. If that is a shop cup, it walked."

"Thank you," he said. "Keep your hands visible, please."

Nina raised her chin. "We need to remove the books," she said. "For the children."

Asa gave her one polite look and then the flat one he uses when the world tries to make him choose the wrong priority. "The books did not pour the tea," he said. "Please stand back."

I keep a small tray on the bar for overflow cups that need a landing. When Rafi set it out earlier, I made a mental note about the odd cup with the starburst glaze. Now I looked at the tray again. Five cups in the plain glossy set. One empty spot. The saucer stack held five for the set, none for the old cup. I looked in the bus bin under the sink. No saucer there. I put that question on a hook in my head.

"Ledger," Asa said, stepping in. "Entry status."

"Clean," I said. "Opening line in blue ballpoint in Rafi's hand. No add-ons. No corrections."

Rafi held it up. Asa glanced, photographed, handed it back. "Keep it under the counter," he said. "Camera on it. Hands off unless we make an entry with a witness."

"Understood," I said.

The alley air shifted. People always feel the temperature change when a day decides it is not going to behave. Paula kept the children picking out sprinkles for imaginary cupcakes. Bria boxed two bars for a mother with a stroller and did not look at the ground again. Martin checked his phone and moved in a small pattern that made no sense to anyone who does not watch how people move when they want to look helpful without touching anything.

"Tea sources," Asa said.

"Two," I said. "Tent urn with peppermint. Shop kettle with peppermint. Same tin. Same batch. I brewed both. The tent set stayed boxed until ten thirty. I saw Bria break the tape twenty minutes before we opened."

Rafi nodded. "I have the tape in the bin if you want the timing."

Asa lifted his head and took in the crowd again. "Anyone leave the tent line and rejoin near the urn when the alley cleared," he asked.

Nina opened her mouth to volunteer someone who would make a convenient headline. I cut her off with a look. She closed her mouth and pretended she had been about to cough.

The church clock on the corner tower gave the quarter. The sound hung in the alley like a simple system that still works.

Harold did not move.

Paramedics eased in with a stretcher and calm hands. They moved with their own rhythm. Asa stepped back and let them take the lead.

I looked from the odd cup bag to the tray at the bar, to the tent, to the banned table, to the ledger in Rafi's hands. The day had set its fuse. It takes no talent to predict an explosion. It takes nerve to stay in the room when it happens and write down what the pieces say.

Sylvie Tran held up her phone and took one wide shot of the alley that captured the tent, the crowd, the donor on the ground, the banned table inside the shop, and the cat on the counter. She lowered the phone and looked at me. "Caption," she said. "One sentence."

"Keep it factual," I said. "Man collapsed at charity bake. Investigation underway. Shop remains open."

She nodded. "You will hate the comments," she said.

"I always do," I said. "Keep them clean."

She nodded again and stepped back.

Asa lifted the bagged cup, held it to eye level, and looked through the plastic at the crazed glaze. He does not pretend to be a ceramics expert. He knows what he is looking for. He turned the bag without letting his fingers touch the rim. He saw what I saw. Old glaze. Crazing. A hairline at the handle. A tide line a touch higher than the tent set would leave.

He lowered the bag and glanced at the tray by the bar. "Overflow cup gone," he said, to himself as much as to me.

"Gone," I said.

Peppermint stood on his hind legs and touched the tray with one paw as if offering corroboration. I scratched his head once and he settled.

Harold's face changed. The paramedics moved. They worked. They spoke to Asa in soft tones. Asa nodded and wrote two numbers in his small book.

The crowd shifted again, this time with the tired movement of people who have been holding a breath for too long and want permission to let it go. Asa gave it to them.

"Thank you for your patience," he said. "If you saw anything unusual near the tea or the back door, come inside and speak with me or with Ms. Wren. We will keep this corner clear. We will keep the day steady."

He looked at me next. "Cup first," he said. "Then the sets."

"Already lined up," I said.

"And the ledger," he said.

"Under camera," I said.

He nodded once. It looked like a tiny bow. He turned to the paramedics and stepped into their rhythm.

Inside, the shop held its breath. The banned table still looked like a reading list. The placards still read like a spine. The espresso bar hummed at a setting that calms rooms. The overflow tray had a hole where an old cup belonged. The ledger's first line sat neat in blue. That line would matter more than I wanted it to.

Harold's last image for the town would be the raised teacup with the banned sign behind him and a cat on a table like a disapproving uncle. The photo would look like a poster. The caption would tell a smaller story. The real story would live in the glaze of a cup, the tilt of a ledger line, a sticky note's ink, and a jacket pocket that should have been empty and was not.

I put my hand on the counter to keep myself from moving too fast. Then I lifted the tray and took it to the sink. The starburst cup was in a bag. Five glossy cups stood in a row. Five saucers waited. One saucer for the odd cup was still missing. I looked at the lost and found box near the espresso grinder and saw a sliver of pale ceramic under a receipt pad. A chipped saucer winked at me like a coin dropped from someone who did not want to be seen paying. I left it there for now. We were not ready to keep it.

Outside, the paramedics lifted. Inside, Bria wiped a nonexistent crumb from her card with the same tenderness she uses on her bakery case. Paula stacked three donated paperbacks on the counter and wrote a small note for the board about context signage. Martin watched his phone.

Nina raised her camera again and took one last photo of the banned table through the glass as if distance gave her claim a halo. The lens caught her reflection and Peppermint's tail in the same rectangle. The town would read meaning into both and be wrong about one.

I turned the placard beside the memoir two degrees to the left so the quote lined straight under the title. I do not like crooked words on a day that already wants to tilt.

"Rafi," I said.

"Got it," he said. "Ledger locked. Tea tins logged. Tent cups accounted for. Overflow count at six, minus one."

He set the ledger in the cradle under the register, checked the camera angle, and looked at me. We keep rooms steady by doing small things exactly right. Today would need a lot of small things.

Harold had raised a cup for a photo. That moment was already on three phones. If the town wanted to produce a story with a villain in the first act, it would pick from the usual list. The loud

PTA chair. The flashy baker. The librarian with a grudge. The spouse in a blazer. The display with a placard that says why. The cat. People are lazy. Evidence is not.

I moved the pen cup closer to the register. Ballpoints only. Gel pens belong at the counter only when I am watching. I knew that before today. Today would prove it again.

The tent flapped once in a gust and settled. The bell chimed as a latecomer opened the front door and stopped cold at the shape the day had taken. I met his eyes, gave him a simple line, and handed him a list of titles and a cookie.

"Welcome," I said. "We are still open."

CHAPTER 2

Bake Tent Bustle

The alley fills like it always does when flour and sugar take charge. Music from a small speaker settles on the bunting in a bright, thin thread. Two juniors from the high school tune a guitar and miss the same note twice, then find it. The mixer from the church kitchen hums in the hall next door and then stops. The tent skin snaps once in a gust and goes slack again. Card tables line up in a neat grid. The tablecloths are off-white with a print of tiny green leaves. It is the kind of pattern old ladies buy in bulk and younger people only notice after they have already put down their cash.

Rafi sets our jar in the center and tapes it to the plastic so the wind does not solve anyone's math. Coins look good in the morning. People want to hear themselves help.

Bria puts her trays out like she is setting diamonds. She smiles, tips her chin toward the light, smooths the wax paper with the back of her fingers, and reads her card out loud as if the ink might wander if she does not. "Bria's Citrus Bars." The lemon sits bright under the powdered sugar and winks. She lines the edges with a knife and dusts the top again with a practiced hand. A teenager in a hoodie stands at the edge of the table and tries to negotiate for a second sample. Bria refuses sweetly and hands him a napkin to save his shirt. He calls her ma'am and blushes.

Paula lifts a covered plate out of a cooler and sets it on the reading guide rack we dragged into the shade. Her hair is how it always is, tucked and sensible. Her eyes move like a scanner. She knows where the children are, where the parents have drifted, and where the pot of tea sits. She points a mother with a stroller toward shade and a chair.

Near the back door, Harold takes up the kind of position that lets him catch three conversations at once. He has a small plate with a pecan square on it and a napkin he does not need. He wears the blazer he wore inside and the same tie that appears in half the town's donation photos. People touch his elbow and he touches theirs back. He tells someone he will match the next basket if the jar hits a hundred before noon. He tells someone else the shop smells like his grandmother's house, which is his way of saying the cinnamon is doing its job.

The tea urn from the church sits at the corner of the tent. Steam moves in a tight column that looks innocent and is not. I brewed the peppermint and moved it outside because mothers with children prefer outside for anything that spills. Beside that, on a secondary table, sits the tray the high schoolers will ferry between tent and shop if demand spikes. On the bar inside I kept the overflow tray for cups that needed a landing during a crush. I kept it there because I know my room and the way people who mean well reach in and put things where they fit in the moment. The matched tent set lives in its crate until it is needed. White cups, white saucers, all in a neat stack. I checked the crate when we opened. Everything matched. It keeps my brain quiet to know that.

Nina has already placed herself halfway between the tent and the front window because she knows cameras want contrast. She holds her tote tight against her body like a shield. She smiles for the person with the feed and frowns at everyone else. Her mouth moves a lot. Her eyes move more.

"Tea is free," Rafi calls. "Put something in the jar if you can."

I pour a cup for a grandmother with a bun like a walnut and another for a father who came straight from work in his paint shirt. The line flows. A small boy on tiptoes asks for a lemon bar and points at powdered sugar smears on four separate napkins. Bria offers him half of a corner and he beams like a lighthouse.

Harold works the crowd. He looks at the placards inside every time he turns toward the window. He looks at the jar every time he faces the tent. He cannot help himself. He cares about numbers as if they were a kind of weather.

Martin hovers near the espresso bar inside. He checks his phone. He comments on the pastry rack. He says the espresso smells fine for a bake sale morning. He laughs when a teenager bumps the counter. He keeps his hands clean.

The two juniors find a rhythm. They sing a song about a boat that leaves and never comes back. Their headphones hang off their necks like medals. The sound makes a thin roof over the alley and holds our little world together.

The crowd crests a little before noon. Families move like schools of fish. Strollers have a way of finding one another at the exact corner that will block a wheel. The jar fills with quarters. The Square reader chirps for cards. The bills get folded and tucked under the jar the way people do when they do not want anyone to count their care.

I step out of the shop with a tray of cups and a fresh pot. Peppermint chooses that moment to climb the step stool near the door and look at me like he has always run the tent. Rafi moves him to the poetry crate. He stays, offended, then forgets he is offended when a child with a cookie puts out a hand.

Harold stops at Bria's table and buys one lemon bar. He lifts it and smells it the way people smell childhood when they are lucky. He puts it on his plate with the pecan square and walks the five steps to the tea urn.

He does not ask me for help. He does not need help. He has poured more cups in this town than some people have read books. He sets his plate down, lifts the tap, and fills to two fingers below the rim. He smiles. He inhales. He turns his shoulder toward the light at the edge of the tent because he knows a good photo angle when he feels one.

Phones rise. Two from the school. One from Sylvie Tran. One from someone I do not know with a case full of glitter. Harold raises his cup for the shot. The banned table sits in the background inside, with Peppermint like a sentry in fur. If you were writing a story with a poster, this is the moment you would print.

He takes a sip. He smiles at the taste the way a person smiles at a song they do not need to learn. He takes a second sip.

His hand shifts as if the air got heavier. The cup tips. The rim slides across his lower lip. The cup leaves his fingers as if they forgot their task. The saucer is not there because he did not take a saucer. The cup meets the ground with the soft thock porcelain makes on hard surface when it does not shatter. It rolls once under the lip of the table. His knees find the pavement. His shoulder follows. His cheek settles on the thin grit that lives in the alley no matter how often the church volunteer mops.

People freeze. They always do. The human brain keeps more silence in it than a shop floor does.

"Twelve fourteen," I say out loud. I do it for the room and for myself. Time keeps a chain clean. "Rafi, call Asa."

"On it," he says. He has the phone out before I finish the sentence. His thumb moves. He says the words with the right order and the right calm. "Peppermint Cat alley. Collapse. Breathing. Need you."

Two high schoolers stand in the way of everything for a half second. Then they lift the bunting and hold it like a curtain so the little ones do not push closer. Paula moves the children to the far table and starts an alphabet game about sprinkles. A kind of order returns because she brings it with her.

I kneel by Harold. The air over him is warmer than the air

over me. The lines at the corner of his eyes soften. A tremor runs along his jaw. He is conscious enough to hear me, not sure enough to answer. I do not touch the cup. My eyes know where it went. I find it with my gaze under the stool foot. It sits on its side, half under shade, half in sun. The glaze catches the light and tells me more than I want it to tell.

The cup is not from the tent set. Not white, not clean heavy glaze, not the identical curve I unpacked and counted. The cup shows a fine starburst of crazing in the finish, a map of hairlines like frost on a window. An old piece that would sit in our thrift mix inside, not in the matched crate Bria brought. The handle carries a faint shadow along one side where the crack has darkened with years of tea and soap.

There is a tide line inside, a thin stain from many lived mornings. It sits a hair higher than the lines inside the tent cups. I do not have those tent cups next to me in this breath, but I packed them, and I have that picture in my head, and this line is higher. Not by much. Enough to sit in my notes. Enough to make me think I will be naming this cup later.

"Keep clear," I say to the front of the circle. I keep my voice steady, not loud. People obey a steady voice.

Nina moves closer instead. She angles her body so Sylvie's phone sees her profile against the shop window. She holds a tissue to her nose and speaks in short cuts that make cameras happy and rooms tired.

"This display poisoned the mood," she says to the phone and the world. "We said it would. We said it would bring harm. The shop insisted."

Sylvie does not answer. She holds the shot. Her eyes flick to me and back. She will edit later. For now she needs clean sound and faces that tell stories people think they already know.

"Paula," I say. "Ledger."

"In hand," she says from the door, and raises the book so I can see it. The first line sits in Rafi's neat hand. Blue ballpoint, time, title, zero. No add-ons. No edits. She keeps it under the counter in the cradle where our camera can see it without glare. She is a librarian who understands where records live and how they die.

Bria stands two steps back from her trays, hands lifted at shoulder height, fingers splayed in reflex. She looks like a baker who just learned knives cut in two directions.

"I did not bring any of your cups out here," she says to me, because I am the person who would know. "My crate stayed shut until ten thirty. We used tent cups only. I can show you the crate tape."

"You will," I say. "Not yet."

Her eyes gather water and stop short of tears. She sucks in air and finds the smile people use when they do not want to frighten children. She hands a napkin to a woman who is shivering in a cardigan and does not know why.

A child with a lollipop asks if the man is sleeping. Paula tells him the man is resting and will hear a siren and then a voice, in that order. The child accepts this and goes back to the sprinkle game. As a town, we know how to follow a calm adult into simple sentences when the hour asks for that skill.

The guitar stops. The juniors look at their hands. One puts the strap over his neck and takes it off again, as if the strap has become a live thing he does not want to insult.

From inside the shop, the espresso machine breathes. Martin appears in the doorway. He does not step into the alley. He looks down at Harold and then at the cup and then at Bria and then at the banned table. He lifts his phone and lowers it without taking a picture. He pockets it and pulls it back out. He wears the same blazer he wore in the last ten committee photos he posted on the church site. He is the kind of person who dresses like a reason.

Rafi steps back into my line of sight. "Asa is two minutes," he says. "Clinic stop at the corner. He was already close."

"Good," I say. "Grab two cones from the storeroom. Set them at the alley mouth."

He moves. He sets the cones. He returns with a roll of pastry string and a piece of chalk. He knows the shape of my mind and where I will put things he has not yet seen.

I keep my hands off the cup. I do not need to touch it to see what it is. The crazing is unique. You can tell one old cup from another if you look long enough. The star lines do not repeat. They branch in the way a watercolor spreads. This set belongs to the shop, not the tent. The tent cups are matched and smooth. The old cup has a story.

Asa steps into the alley. He looks first at Harold, then at me, then at the cup, then at the crowd. He moves with a stance that says he can hear three conversations and a kettle at the same time. He kneels by Harold, checks for breath and pulse, speaks to him in a low voice that means yes, the words will get in even if the brain is not ready to shape them.

"Time," he says, eyes still on Harold.

"Twelve fourteen," I say.

He nods. He stands. He looks at the cup. "Point," he says.

I point. He lowers his bag to the ground, draws a clear sleeve, slides it under the rim of the cup, and lifts with the gentleness of someone who has dropped his own dishes and learned the hard way how to pick them up without losing the last of what they can tell. He seals the sleeve at the top and writes the time and the place and the item on the strip. He sets the sleeve on the table and lifts his phone for three photos. Rim, handle, inside curve. He does not need to name what I see. He sees it too.

"Not tent stock," he says.

"Shop stray," I say. "Old glaze. Starburst crazing. Missing saucer this morning at my sink."

"Where did the saucer go," he says.

"Not sure," I say. "I will check lost and found when you give me a breath."

He tips the sleeve to the light and we both catch the faint tea tide line inside. I know where the tent cups caught their line this morning when I tested fill levels. This sits higher. The difference is enough to notice once you decide to notice and cannot decide not to.

Nina takes the opening she thinks he gave her and faces the ring. "You see what a display like this does," she says. "It poisons a day. I said it would. People laughed. Who is laughing now."

Sylvie keeps her camera steady and raises an eyebrow that reads stop. Nina does not see the eyebrow. She makes her mouth into a small line of victory and holds her tote like a book she plans to assign to the town. People farther back roll their eyes and look at their feet. People closer in do not look at her at all.

Bria goes pale. "My cups never touched your tray," she says to me, low, for me and only me. "I kept my crate by my table. My staff knows better than to mix sets. I count cups like I count eggs."

"I know," I say. "Let me do the counting now."

She nods fast. She folds her hands under the table so the children will not see them shaking.

Paula still has the ledger under the counter. She holds it like a baby bird. She watches me and waits for a cue. She does not give me notes I did not ask for. I keep that for later when I have room for her sharp eye and not before.

The paramedics arrive. The guitar players step back the way a tide goes out when a boat pulls in. The paramedics do their job. Asa speaks to them and writes two numbers on his card. He looks at me, and the look holds a lot of town and a lot of years and a lot of the kind of trust you cannot print.

"Sets," he says.

"In the crate," I say. "Let me show you."

We walk to the tent table where the crate sits under Bria's sign. I kneel, lift the lid, and show the stack. White cups, white saucers, no crazing, no hairlines, no missing piece. I count in a whisper. Ten cups. Ten saucers. One in use at the urn. Two on the table in hands. One at the far end on a chair somebody used as a table.

23

That makes fourteen. The crate holds eight. The count matches the last number I wrote on my prep sheet. The loose cup in the sleeve on Asa's table makes fifteen, but it belongs to the wrong family.

"Your cup walked," he says.

"From the shop," I say. "From the overflow tray. I left that tray on the bar for bustle. I should have tucked it behind the espresso machine. I will whip myself later."

He does not smile. He does not frown. He nods. He writes. He points. Rafi steps in and circles the space where the cup lay with pastry string and chalk so anyone passing through later will know where it was. The string grid is one of the small habits we teach the juniors who help on event days. This keeps them from moving things. This keeps us from trusting our memory when we are tired.

Inside, the front table with banned titles sits under calm light. Peppermint has claimed one corner as if he filed a notice. He licks his paw and wipes his face with the rhythm of a metronome. He is a cat who thinks a shop should be set to his schedule. He is not wrong much of the time.

Martin hovers in the doorway and watches the alley and the tray and the cup in the sleeve. He looks at Nina and then away. He looks at Bria and nods. He looks at the ledger and looks away fast because he would rather you think he does not care about entries and ink and totals.

Asa speaks to the paramedics. They lift. They shift. They move. They ride their own river, and when they decide where to take it, they do not ask the room for votes. Harold leaves in an orderly way that we can live with. The alley exhales the breath it has been holding since twelve fourteen.

Rafi hands me a roll of absorbent towels and a bucket. "For the puddle," he says. There is no puddle. There is only a light crescent of tea that will stain if we ignore it. I blot the mark and leave the rest for later when my head is not carrying a count and a calendar and every face people use when they tell themselves a story they want to believe.

A mother approaches Bria and asks for two bars in a paper bag. Bria thanks her more than the bars are worth because she needs to do something besides watch the table where the cup had been.

I pull my phone and check the time again out of habit. Twelve twenty-two. It feels like a different hour than the one on the wall clock over the church door. Events bend minutes. People pretend they do not. I write both times in a small notebook so I can argue with myself later and win.

Nina raises her volume because no one gave her a microphone. She tells a woman from the yoga studio that the display is to blame. She tells an older man with a hat full of pins that our shop refuses to consider families. She tells anyone who will take the bait that the town wanted an argument and the shop provided one. She plants her feet near the jar as if the jar were a pulpit.

No one engages her. They have enough to hold today without her. She will tell her thread later that she spoke for the children and the town shrugged. She will like that story. She will post three photos and none of them will show that the cup had star lines and a missing saucer and a life before today.

I pick up the sleeve with the cup and look again at the glaze. The crazing looks like a frost pattern from a pond near the courthouse. If I had to match it, I could. I do not have to. I know the piece. It has sat on our shelf long enough to feel like one of the shop's small scars.

"Inside," Asa says.

"Inside," I say.

We carry the sleeve to the counter. Paula lowers the ledger into the cradle. Rafi lines up two clean saucers from the tent set next to a cup from the same stack. He puts the shop cup in its sleeve beside them. The contrast does the work without theory or speech. The tent set is straight white. The old cup holds a map of years.

We keep the glass clean because you can see more truth when nothing fogs the pane between you and the object. The camera above the register looks down with the kind of glare you get from a good memory. The top frame holds the tables and the ledger and the cup and the jar and the hands that pass across all four.

The alley still hums. The guitar tries again and finds a lower, kinder tune. The wind slows. The children at the far table draw sprinkles into letters that spell names and cats and a word only one mother can read.

Sylvie lowers her phone and takes a breath. She steps inside and looks at the cup without touching the sleeve. She looks at Paula's hands on the ledger. She looks at the placards again and nods once, like a person who prefers print to clips and is not allowed to pick her medium for a living.

"Caption," she says.

"Keep it clean," I say. "Man collapses at charity bake. Investigation underway. Shop remains open."

"I used that line already," she says. "It works."

"It still works," I say.

She steps back out, spins once to catch the bunting in a quick pan, and posts. Her feed will fill. She will spend the next hour fighting off comments that use three words to do ten jobs. She will delete the worst. She will leave the ones that care about the jar and the guitar and the mother who found shade.

Asa signs the seal on the sleeve and writes a number on the strip. He goes out to speak to Harold's husband. He uses his quiet voice, not the one that scares children. I watch Martin listen. He nods at the right beats. He looks wounded in a way that does not reach his eyes. He offers to help with anything we need and then does not touch a thing. He tells two people they should keep buying bars. He raises his phone to check the time and holds it there longer than time needs.

Nina stops talking long enough to let a woman from the church climb the step and make a short statement about prayer and patience and keeping the alley clear. People breathe easier in the presence of a person who does not try to turn a bad hour into a campaign. Nina waits until the woman steps down and then says to no one and everyone that the display is to blame for public conflict and that she will speak at the next board meeting to protect the children from scenes like this.

The children are drawing sprinkles into stars and cats and cannot hear her. The adults hear and choose to pretend they did not. That is our town at its best and worst.

I turn to the sink and set the two tent cups beside the shop cup. I do not wash them. I want Asa to see them as they are. I make a small note for myself about the missing saucer for the old cup. It has no partner in the tent stack. It has no partner in the cupboard. No dish matches its glaze. It travels alone.

"Rafi," I say.

"Here," he says.

"Write the time on the label for the tent cup stack," I say. "Note that we counted before and after and found the same number minus the two in hands and one on the chair."

"Done," he says.

"Write one line about the old cup's tide line," I say.

"High by a breath," he says, and writes that because he likes the way I phrase things when I mean a small measure and not a number.

A teacher from the middle school steps in and asks for a copy of our placards for her classroom. "For context," she says. She looks at the cup and does not ask for a story. She sees that one exists and knows the hour will share it when it is ready.

I print her a set and sign the bottom so the board will leave her alone for one more week. It will not stop their letters. It will give her a glue point.

Back outside, Nina has found someone new to hear her line. She tells a man in a golf shirt that the display killed the mood. She tells a teen in a fleece that this is what happens when a shop pushes books that do not respect families. She tells a woman with a sleeping baby that she warned everyone and no one listened. The woman with the sleeping baby looks at her, then at the baby, then at the bunting. Nina moves on to a better audience.

Rafi rings the bell on the jar to mark the half hour the way we always do at fundraisers. One clean note against the noise. Coins follow. People like a ritual downbeat. It makes them think they are part of a song, not trapped in a scene. The jar fills again. The tent breathes. The alley remembers it is a place for cake and not for panic.

Inside, Peppermint abandons the poetry crate and returns to the banned table. He puts his head on his paws and watches the door, which is his way of saying I see the line you drew between inside and out and I approve. If he could read, I would let him initial the ledger. He reads in other ways.

Asa comes back in and rests his hand on the counter for a second like he is checking if the wood is as steady as the room. "We will need your camera footage," he says.

"You will have it," I say. "Top frame for the counter and the ledger. Side frame for the bar and the tray. The outside feed for the tent corner and the urn."

"Keep them running," he says.

"They do not sleep," I say.

"And the display," he says, with a look that asks a question without much appetite for the answer.

"It stays," I say. "Context and a chair and tea. No smoke machines. No tricks."

"Good," he says.

He picks up the sleeve and looks once more at the starburst glaze.

He reads the tide line with me without using the words tide or line. He nods to Rafi and to Paula. He looks out at the alley and then back at me.

"Noise will rise," he says.

"I expect that," I say.

"Hold your chain," he says.

"I always do," I say.

He steps aside so a boy with a dollar can put it in the jar without getting near the cup. The boy salutes the cat and runs back to his mother with a grin that feels like a small part of the town decided to keep growing up on schedule.

Outside, Nina repeats herself for anyone who missed her first round. "The display killed the mood," she says, to a couple in line for bars, to a neighbor who walked past with her dog, to a city worker on break with a muffin in a napkin. The dog sneezes and licks a crumb and looks happier than the people. The couple nods and then buys two bars. The worker eats the muffin and stares at the bunting like it never gets old.

In my head, I underline the sentence I will write later. The mood was fine until a cup with a history walked into the tent. The children were fine until an adult decided he needed proof of a point he had not made yet. The books sat in their light and did their quiet work. The alley smelled like peppermint and sugar. The music found a kinder key. The town will remember the line Nina gave them because loud lines stick. I will write the counterline on paper and keep it on a shelf where it can be found by the next person who needs a shape for the truth.

For now, the table is set, the jar sings on the half hour, and a cup in a sleeve sits on my counter like a small animal whose prints we will read when the day stops shaking. Outside, Nina fills the air with the claim she wants to carry home. "The display killed the mood," she says, again and again, and the alley, stubborn and kind, refuses to clap.

CHAPTER 3

Cup Confusion

I took the sleeve with the starburst cup to the espresso bar and set it beside the sink. The counter had that clean morning smell of citrus soap and coffee oils that never quite leave. Rafi pulled the drying rack closer and cleared a strip of steel with two tight swipes of a towel. He knows how my brain works. Give me a line, give me light, give me a place to set pieces in order.

"Count," I said.

"On it," he said.

He brought the tent crate in from the alley and set it on the mat at my feet. He popped the latches and lifted the lid with careful hands. The matched white cups sat nested in pairs, saucers on their side like thin moons. No glaze crazing. No hairlines. No stories in the surface. A rental dream.

I slipped on gloves and set three tent cups in a row next to the sink. Then three matched saucers. Then I pulled three of our shop cups from the high shelf. Our set is a mutt. Thrift finds, estate boxes, the odd gift from a customer who thought porcelain meant love. Five of ours matched in a plain gloss. The sixth did not. The odd one looked like a small pond in winter, the glaze full of star cracks, the handle vein darkened by age and heat.

Rafi watched me line them. Tent, tent, tent. Shop, shop, odd. He put the kettle on the back burner to give us steam if we wanted it. He did not ask questions. He lets me get the shape on the table before he talks.

"Angle," I said.

He shifted the task lamp so a white cone fell across both rows. The matched tent cups showed nothing but clean curve. The shop cups showed tiny scuffs in the glaze. The odd one broke light like spun sugar. Fine crazing everywhere you looked. A tide line inside, a little higher than the line that sits in the tent cups. I could feel the mismatch in my teeth.

"Rafi," I said. "Morning wash, yesterday. Did this sit in your rack."

He peered into the crazing like he was reading a poem you have to hold to the light. He has a better memory for small chores than any person I know. It is why the ledger lines sit straight and our filters get changed on time.

"Yeah," he said. "I grabbed it off the poetry shelf after close. It had a lipstick ghost. Pale coral, not loud. I ran it through the bar sink with the citrus soap, then set it to dry with the plain set. I did not see a saucer."

"Handle," I said.

He leaned closer. The handle carried a hairline on the inside curve where fingers like to pinch. The hairline had gone brown along the crack. Age does that when tea finds a seam. There was a small nick at the foot. If I had to pick this cup out of a lineup, I would not need more than a second.

"Wash temp," I said.

"Hot," he said. "Not enough to craze it. It came to me like that. I noticed the pattern. Thought it was pretty. Thought about throwing it out anyway. Decided not to because the shelf looked low."

I picked the odd cup up in the sleeve and turned it over. No maker's mark left. The crazing would have killed any stamp years ago. The foot ring was smooth in a way that told me hands had set it down on many mornings in many kitchens. This was not a rental life.

"Saucer still missing," I said.

"Check the lost and found," he said.

I opened the lost and found box. A chipped saucer, pale and sorry, lay under a receipt pad. The chip sat at three o'clock like a small bite. The glaze tone matched the odd cup better than the tent porcelain did. I lifted it and held it beside the cup in the sleeve. The fit was not tight, but it belonged to the same story. I wrote that on a card and slid the saucer into a second sleeve.

"Two sleeves," I said. "Odd cup and probable saucer."

Rafi labeled both with time and place. He writes time like he is daring you to misread it.

I turned to the rack and set one tent cup in my palm. Smooth glaze. No memory. It would survive a hundred bake sales and retire without a story. I set it back and put my fingers inside the rim of the odd one, still in the sleeve, feeling the ridge of the tide line through the plastic. The line sat that hair higher than the set. It was a small difference you only see if you stand in this room long enough and pour enough tea for strangers. That is my job.

Bria's voice reached us before she did. She speaks in a bright key even when she is scared. She crossed the threshold and stood on the clean side of the bar like a kid who has been told not to touch the frosting and means to obey.

"Tell me it is not mine," she said.

"It is not yours," I said. "Not tent stock. Ours. Old."

She closed her eyes for one breath, opened them, and pressed her palms flat on the counter. "Thank you," she said. "It sat in the sleeve like it had my name on it."

"The crate held," I said. "Your lids stayed on. We will pull your tape in a minute and log the times. For now, look."

I pointed to the row. Tent, tent, tent. Shop, shop, odd. Bria leaned in until her nose almost touched the sleeve. She is good with sugar, and sugar teaches people to notice small changes. Her face relaxed by a notch. She saw it. Smooth glaze versus the dense star map. Family versus orphan.

"That hairline," she said. "That is not today's work."

"That is thousands of mornings," I said. "The handle carried a crack before we unboxed at ten. No way it came out of your crate. Your set lives in a rental office most days. They do not let old pieces near their invoices."

She nodded. She backed up half a step and took her hands off the counter. She is a person who knows when not to spread prints.

"Who brought it out," she said.

"That is the next card," I said.

Rafi flipped back through his mental roll. He saw his hands last night, the rack, the towel. He saw me this morning shifting cups from shelf to tray. He saw Peppermint sniff the odd one and turn away. He saw the overflow tray move two inches to make room for a plate with a scone Rafi had not meant to eat, then saw him eat it anyway. He saw a hand he could not place lift a white matching cup and set it on the tray. He did not see anyone take the odd one. That is why cameras matter.

"Bar cam will show the tray," he said. "Top cam will show the ledger. Side cam will see the pass between bar and tent. If the cup walked, it walked past those two eyes."

I took a bright cloth and ran it under the rim of one tent cup and one of our plain shop cups to compare residue. The tent glaze flashed water clean. Our plain cup held a smudge that caught on the cloth thread. I marked the cloth with a dot in the corner so I would not pretend later that I did not see what I saw.

"Soap," Rafi said. "Citrus clear on the tent cups. House mix on ours. The odd one got citrus yesterday, but the glaze eats everything and still looks like winter."

He is right. Old crazing drinks. You can scrub until your shoulders shake and the lines will still hold the ghosts of old mornings. I took the loupe and put it on the inner wall of the odd cup through the sleeve. The star lines went where fine cracks go. Not a flaw from firing. A flaw from years.

Paula stepped in behind Bria and watched without speaking. She keeps a librarian's distance until asked.

"Stand here," I said to her, moving her to the camera's gaze. "Witness for the count."

She nodded and set her bag on the stool and took out a pen. Not a gel. A black archival with a precise tip. She dated the page and wrote three lines in a tight hand. Tent cups, three. Shop cups, three. Odd cup, star crazing, sleeve one. Saucer, chipped, sleeve two.

I appreciate a scribe who does not make a speech.

"Saucer lived in the lost and found box," I said. "Under a receipt pad. No tape, no label. It landed there last night or this morning. We will check the time on the camera that watches this side of the bar."

"Why would a person bring a shop cup out to the tent," Bria asked, more to the air than to me. "The crate lives two steps from the urn. Convenience does not explain it. Nothing explains it unless you want something that does not belong on camera."

Paula hummed a small yes and kept writing.

Rafi brought the crate closer and set one tent saucer beside the odd saucer. He put his finger on the lip where the chip sat. "This one chipped on the inside curve," he said. "Most chips from the alley show on the outer ring. This came from a quick knock against a counter. Not a fall from height."

"Which counter," I said.

He glanced at the edge of our sink. The stainless lip has a tiny nick about a thumb's width long. It has been there for months. It is exactly the kind of place where a person who is not thinking will rattle a saucer and take a bite out of it without noticing. He looked at the angle of the chip again, then at the nick. "Possible," he said. He will not overstate a match. I like that about him.

"Either way," I said. "Saucer is ours, not tent stock."

Paula wrote that down.

I brought the odd cup closer and peered at the handle foot through the sleeve. The hairline sat like a note on a staff. Old. It had been there yesterday. Rafi's wash would not have made it. The crazing had been there yesterday. My eye would not have missed it because it is the kind of flaw I file without trying. The tide line sat higher than the tent set by a hair. That would matter later when people tried to say all cups look the same and liquid finds its own level in any room.

Bria pointed at the odd cup and then at the tent set. "That one does not belong in anything I brought," she said. "And I did not put a shop cup on my table. I count. I counted when I broke the tape. I counted when I set the stack. I counted after the fall."

"Say it on record," I said.

She spoke toward the side camera. "I did not put a shop cup on my table. My set stayed boxed until ten thirty. My staff did not pull from the bar. The only time anyone grabbed a cup not from my crate was when a mother asked for a lid and I told her we had none."

Her voice shook once and then held. She has stage legs from bakes and fairs. They serve her now.

Rafi closed the crate and slid it under the counter. He pulled the overflow tray forward. The plain set from the shop sat with one gap. Five cups, not six. Five saucers, not six. The gap lined up where the odd one had lived this morning. I had moved it back two inches from Peppermint's paw. That memory sat in my shoulder. It sat in Rafi's too. He pointed at the blank spot like a chess player marking the square where a knight should be.

"Here," he said. "This is where it sat. I remember because I wiped under it and left a ring I planned to polish out later."

He lifted the tray and showed me the ring, faint and perfect. I took a photo and slid the tray back into place. The camera over the bar would have that tray in shot all morning. Good.

I opened the cupboard and pulled the shop saucers one by one to check for a match to the chipped one. None. The odd saucer was alone. I slid it back into its sleeve and sealed it.

Paula finished her notes and set the pad aside. "You are building a map," she said.

"I am building a list," I said. "Maps pretend you know where you are going. Lists help you find your way back when the hour pushes you around."

She smiled. "You will get your promotion," I said, because I knew what last month had cost her.

She pressed her lips together and nodded once. "Today is not about me," she said.

"Today is about a cup," I said.

We all stood a little closer to the counter and looked at the starburst.

Bria ran a finger over the rim of one tent cup, then pulled her hand back when she remembered the camera. "Someone wanted the old one in play," she said. "Why else swap."

"Or wanted it all to look like a crush and grabbed the nearest cup without knowing the tent crate was two steps away," Paula said.

"Or wanted to move a cup that had something from the shelf to the alley," I said.

We let each idea sit. None of them were proof. All of them belonged on a board for later.

Rafi moved to the monitor and pulled the bar cam to the last hour. I watched over his shoulder while he scrubbed the timeline. The tray sat in the frame. The overflow set lined it like a piano. Peppermint popped up and sniffed. I pulled him away and set him on poetry. I moved the tray two inches because his tail wanted to claim a cup. Rafi wiped under one foot and left the faint ring. We watched three customers take espresso and return cups. We watched a teenager return a saucer to the wrong stack and Rafi fix it. We watched a hand we did not know yet reach for the tray and set a shop cup on the bar top while Bria took her crate to the tent for the first time. Not the odd cup. One of the plain five. The hand wore no ring. The sleeve looked like a spray jacket. Could be anyone. The shot did not show the face. Rafi backed up the clip and saved the time.

"Later," I said. "We pull all angles once the room stops shaking."

Asa stepped behind us and watched the row of cups. He does not like fussy displays, but he trusts my method because it makes his job easier.

"Split the sets," he said.

"Done," I said. "Tent cups on the left. Shop on the right. Odd in the sleeve. Saucer in a second sleeve. Missing saucer in cupboard, none. Lost and found sleeve added."

He nodded and took two photos without getting the lamp glare. Then he leaned in at the same angle I had used. He looked at the tide line, not at the glaze. He has learned over years when to pretend he does not know the answer and when to show that he does.

"Handle hairline," he said.

"Grew up in someone's kitchen," I said.

He looked at Bria. "Your tape."

"It held," she said. "You can peel it off yourself."

"I will," he said. "Not now."

Bria bit her lip. "Say again that it is not mine," she said to me.

"It is not yours," I said, steady. "Your set stayed boxed. Your lids stayed on. Your tray did not take the odd cup's shape because it does not belong to your line. The glaze on this one tells its own age."

She exhaled and put a hand flat on the counter to ground herself. She needed a task. I gave her one.

"Bring me your crate inventory sheet," I said. "We will staple it to a copy of the time we broke the tape. Then you can go back to the tent and sell sugar to people who need to forget Nina."

Bria smiled at that and left in a hurry.

Paula lingered. She has questions in her eyes she will file for later. For now she watches the sink and the sleeve and the row under the lamp. She knows the line about context works for more than books.

"Who had a reason to touch the bar tray," she said.

"Everyone," Rafi said. "It sits by the register. It invites hands."

"Who had a reason to pick a shop cup over a tent cup," she said.

"Someone moving too fast," I said. "Or someone who entered from the shop side. Or someone who wanted the old cup near the alley because it held more than tea."

We let that sit too. There is no need to say poison when your nose can smell the mint and your brain can do the rest. Asa does not like big words in rooms where people can hear them. I save them for the office.

I took a breath and counted the pieces again. Tent, tent, tent. Shop, shop. Odd. Saucer chipped. Saucer missing from cupboard. Tray ring. Handle hairline. Tide line high. Rafi's memory of lipstick coral. My memory of Peppermint's whiskers. Bria's voice saying she did not mix sets. The camera eye that would break any story into frames we can live with.

I wrote the count on a card and slotted it behind the register in the little box where I keep phrases that need to stay true for the next hour. It keeps me from rewriting the past when the present squeezes.

Bria returned with the crate sheet and the tape tail. She set them on the counter with a neat slap. "There," she said. "Box seamed at ten twelve. Opened at ten thirty. No hands in the gap. I had the box under my elbow the whole time."

"Staple that," I said to Rafi.

He did. He dated the corner.

Bria touched the sleeve with the back of her knuckle and pulled away like she had encountered a live wire. "My set stayed boxed until the tent opened," she said. "Swear it."

"Sworn," I said.

She lifted her chin and spoke toward the ceiling, toward the camera, toward anyone who would try to fold her into a story she did not belong in. "My set stayed boxed until the tent opened," she said again, clean and loud. Then she went back to the alley to put sugar on plates and calm on faces.

CHAPTER 4

Ballot Batch

The counter took the weight of the night the way old wood does. It did not groan. It held. I set the lockbox key beside the stack of ivory slips and told my hands to behave. Touch what you need. Leave the rest for Asa.

"Filled ballots first," I said. "Blank to the side."

Rafi slid a tray under my elbow so nothing would slide to the floor. Gran stationed herself where she could see paper and people at the same time. Margo stayed in her chair, posture tall, eyes in that soft neutral she uses when she wants to look helpful. Jenna kept one palm flat on her lap as if muscles learn from warnings. Conrad watched the door and pretended that counted as work.

Peppermint leapt to the far end of the counter, sat like a small statue, and blinked at the stack. He likes paper with plans attached.

I lifted the top slip. The weight felt right for a downtown stationer, not the thin stuff we keep for receipts. A faint oval leapt when I tilted it under the pendant. Cat's eye. I knew it with my thumb before I named it. Gran's old donation ream, the one the law firm dumped when they switched brands. We tore through that during Blind Date Night last year. I remember because the wrappers ran smooth across twine and did not tear when people yanked at the reveal.

"Watermark," I said.

Gran leaned in. "Cat's eye," she said, not loud and not a question. "We used the last quire by June."

"Every sheet," I said. I worked the stack like a dealer cutting a deck. Mark on the first. Mark on the second. Mark on the third. It kept going. All the slips Margo had brought wore that oval when light hit the grain. No mix. No accident. Someone collected and saved what should have been gone.

Rafi lifted the filled ones free with tongs from the repair kit and set them in a clean tray. He has food service habits that survive any crisis. He does not touch a thing he does not have to touch. He does not smudge ink and then explain it later.

"Names," Asa said from my left. He had moved close enough to hear and far enough not to loom.

"No names on the face," I said. "The club rule was blind slips. But I know the stack. This came from inside our world."

Gran nodded. "We loaned the last of that ream to the club before June," she said. "Margo signed out the leftovers after Blind Date Night. She said she would return what we did not use. I put a sticky on the ledger. I can fetch it."

"No one leaves," Asa said, gentle. "Tell me what the sticky says. I can fetch the page later."

Gran did not fumble. "The sticky says, Margo picked up two packs of cat's eye wrappers and one sleeve of slips," she said. "She took them home after the party. She promised to bring back what remained. She did not."

Margo made a small, contained smile. "I keep club supplies together," she said. "No harm in being organized."

"Where do you keep them," I said.

"In the club bin," she said.

"We do not have a club bin," I said.

"At my place," she said, fast correction. "A plastic tote. I bring it when we need it."

"As a rule," Asa said, "people tell me about bins after the fact. People who like control like bins."

Margo pressed her lips together without losing her smile. "Structure keeps peace," she said.

"Structure owned by one person does not," Gran said.

I slid the last filled slip into the tray and picked up the blank that had lived at the bottom of the stack. It had a mark at the corner. A faint brown ring sat half on the paper and half where air had been. Rings like that come from glass that does not get cleaned. Ours has a ghost ring near the top left, the one I always mean to scrub when days give me more than sixty seconds. This ring had a tiny notch at two o'clock, a chip in the curve, like someone had set a mug down too hard, then lifted before the drip spread. Our ring has no notch. Council's does. I see that glass when I copy meeting notices. The chamber copier carries a coffee stain with a chip in the arc and a hairline scratch that catches toner when you print too near the edge.

I turned the sheet under the lamp until the notch caught light. There it was. Not a perfect circle. A circle with a bite.

"Gran," I said. "Look at the corner."

She moved beside me and frowned, the way she does when a bibliography lies. "Not ours," she said. "Ours is a full ring. Council's copier has a chip. This one has the chip."

Margo brightened for a blink. "Problem solved," she said. "If the chamber copier did it, that means the slips were printed there. The club holds meetings in the council room sometimes. Nothing to do with me."

I shook my head. "You brought the pack tonight," I said. "The pack rode that glass before it came here. The coffee ring mark sits on the bottom sheet of your stack. It rode there at the time it was copied or printed. It did not arrive there in a dream."

Asa took a photo of the corner and another of the watermark. He did not narrate his work. He stamped time in his head. He will check the camera later against the clock and against the router log. He will pull the chamber maintenance reports if he needs to.

"Where did you print the question," he asked Margo.

"In my office," she said.

I tapped the notch. "This is chamber glass," I said. "Not shop. Not your home printer. You carried this stack where the copier has a coffee stain with a chip."

She looked right at me and tried a mild blink I suppose works on people who want to be soothed. "You are mistaken," she said. "I typed the question at my desk."

"Typing is not printing," I said.

Rafi made a small sound that meant he wanted to be helpful. "We do not lend the back copier," he said. "We keep the lid taped at night. The key for that tape lives on Liora's chain."

Asa looked at the blank again. "We will go to the chamber after we finish here," he said. "We will look at the glass. For tonight, this tells me where the stack passed, not who carried it. We pair it with the ledger sticky and the watermark and see whose version bends."

I set the blank down and slid the full tray toward Asa. He did the bag-and-tag rhythm that calms me down. He wrote Ballot slips, filled, count eighteen. He wrote Source: moderator's pack on counter at twelve oh eight per witness. He wrote watermark present on face of each. He did not write opinions on the label. Labels do not want to carry anyone's feelings.

Peppermint stood, put a single toe on the tray's lip, and withdrew it. Boundaries respected.

"We are not voting," Conrad said, half to himself, half to the room. He sounded like a man who has realized the contract will sit for months and hates paper for making him wait. "This whole circus for nothing."

"Not nothing," Gran said. "We learned what paper the circus rides."

"Erica has nothing," he said, low. "She has a cousin who runs the rent and a group she tried to hold together. This is the kind of room where the people with tools decide who gets to sit."

I let him talk. He was not wrong. He was also not the one who would set the frame tonight.

Asa looked at the lockbox key, then at the timer phone on the table beside it. "Device names," he said to me, not loud.

"ME-TAB joined at eleven fifty-five," I said. "It toggled the smart bulbs in a group called Front Row twice on the admin page at twelve and at five past. Our wall rocker was still down. The wheel timer near the breaker is off. Rafi never touched it."

Margo gave me that pitying smile again. "You do not understand how smart bulbs fluctuate," she said.

"I understand how logs write," I said. "They record their own little history whether we ask or not."

"The app on my phone is for home lamps," she said. "You are reading the wrong line."

"You can show me your tablet later," Asa said. "For now, hold your seat. We are still on paper."

I lifted the lockbox key and set it on the tray lip that Peppermint had touched. Small visual rules help. People behave with props. I picked up the top filled slip and looked at the graphite. Most lines read Yes for discussion next week. No one had written a name. One hand had pressed far harder than the rest, marks denting the paper below. Hard pressure tends to live in hands that want control. That is a theory, not a charge. I filed it under tone.

"Count them later," Asa said. "Right now we care about where they came from, not what they say."

"They came from the club bin," Margo said, louder, as if repetition might turn false into true.

"There is no club bin here," I said.

"Then my tote," she said. "You can call it what you like. It exists. The paper sat inside until we needed it."

"And you needed it tonight," Gran said. "A show of order, built out of stock you grabbed from our cupboard last spring and never returned."

Margo stayed with small. "I am a volunteer," she said. "I keep things neat."

"Neat in one person's closet is not neat," Gran said, not rising, not spitting. She could teach classes in how to strip a sentence down to bone.

Asa took the tray, sealed it, wrote the time on the edge, and passed it to his partner. He picked up the bottom blank, took two more shots of the notch in the ring, and slid the sheet into its own sleeve. "Blank with artifact," he said to the partner. "Mark: coffee ring notch consistent with council copier. Bag separate."

Jenna leaned forward. "Does this mean we stop looking at me," she said. "Because I would like that."

"No," Asa said, mild. "It means we keep a clean record that will not help you if you lie again."

She shut her mouth. Good choice.

Benji cleared his throat. "My vote is blank," he said, then flushed like he had confessed to theft. "I did not want to write on paper I did not know."

"You will tell me that again in a quiet room," Asa said, softer. "Thank you."

I stacked the remaining blanks and tied them with twine from the kit. No one would touch them until we understood them. I wrote Ballot blanks, cat's eye, tied by Liora in pencil on a small tag and taped it to the pack. Peppermint put a paw on the knot and gave it a little pat. Quality control.

Margo watched every move. She did not reach. She also did not own the counter anymore. She knew it. Her eyes did a small quick dart, from my hand to the lockbox key, to the phone under Peppermint's paw, to Asa's notes, back to my hand. That is an old tell. People who want control look for the keystone. They rarely pick the right one. Tonight the keystone was not my key. It was the paper that would not lie for her.

"Asa," I said, "we can go to the chamber copier when you are ready. The chip will sit where it sat last week. The notch on this ring will match that bite. I can show you the exact scratch at four o'clock that catches toner."

"We will go," he said. "After I get everyone's first statement."

Margo tried one more throw. "You do not understand the demands of moderation," she said. "People need guidance. They need a clear frame. That is all I tried to give them."

"You tried to give yourself a lever," Gran said, tired and true. "You asked paper to carry it."

Peppermint stood again, stretched, and let out one brief chirp at Margo's sleeve, the slim gray one she keeps by her knee. He has a good sense for where people hide the thing they want to hold. She slid the sleeve farther under her tote with her ankle and pretended the cat had no meaning.

"The pack came from the club bin," she said again, flat.

"There is no club bin here," I said, flat as stone.

Silence did the last work. The tray sat sealed. The bottom blank sat bagged. The lockbox key sat where everyone could see it and no one could claim a mix-up. The pendants hummed. The camera blinked red. The kettle clicked as it lost heat.

"Next," Asa said to me, voice still steady. "Timer check at the back. Then router."

"Break room," I said. "Wheel dial still off."

Margo lifted her chin. "Two seconds helped focus the room," she said to Asa as if that counted as a defense.

"Two seconds helped someone push a chair and knock a ladder loose," he said. "What it did not do was hide where your paper came from."

She smiled without heat. "You think paper will convict me," she said.

He did not smile. "I think paper remembers who carried it," he said.

I slid the twined pack of blanks into a clear sleeve, wrote my initials over the tape, and pushed it into Asa's reach. He took it and did not thank me. He does not thank people for doing what a room requires.

Peppermint lowered his head onto the counter, still watching Margo. His eyes hold green slow fire when he concentrates. He looks like a librarian who knows a patron has not told the truth on a form.

The club bin line lay there like a coin that will not spend. I left it on the floor. Some claims do not need a hammer. They need a vacuum. When the room refuses to believe them, they die on their own.

I palmed the lockbox key and let the metal cool my skin. "We are done with ballots for now," I said. "We move to switches and logs."

Margo said nothing. She did not have a new line. Good. That was the first honest silence I had heard from her all night.

CHAPTER 5

PTA Smoke

The sidewalk took on the look of a small press pool even though no van had shown up and no masthead had given orders. Phones were out. Faces angled toward the shop window where the banned table sat in calm light. The bunting along the bake tent lifted and dropped like a breath. The jar at the corner chimed once for a quarter and once for a key that had missed a pocket.

Sylvie Tran had planted herself where she always plants herself on these days. Not on the step, not blocking the entrance, but just left of the fire lane stripe, back to the window so her camera caught the banner, the tent edge, and the person speaking. She was steady. She had tucked her hair behind one ear. She had the mic clipped to her collar. She kept the lens at chest height instead of the hungry angle you get from people who want a tear more than a sentence.

Nina saw that lens and turned her body so the poster about context would frame her shoulders. She does not need a podium. She carries one inside her voice.

"We warned you," she said to the camera and to every eye that might meet hers. "We said a display like this brings harm into spaces where children should feel safe. Today proves the point. A man fell in front of our sons and daughters. He fell because this shop insists on courting controversy."

She did not look toward the alley. She did not look for Asa. She did not ask if the man had a name beyond donor. She had a speech and a lens. She had the kind of anger that stands like a shield when a person wants to feel useful.

"Say your name for the feed," Sylvie said. She kept her tone neutral. She held the mic like a person who understands that a hand near a mouth makes the story about the hand.

"Nina Carrow," Nina said. "PTA chair. Mother of three. We put on book fairs without this nonsense. The Council needs to step in. Pull the table. Make a policy. Our kids do not need this."

"Our kids need books," a woman said behind me, under her breath, not to pick a fight, but because the sentence wanted air.

Nina kept going. "No one is against reading," she said. "We are for care. We are for protecting childhood. We are for stories that do not poison families against their own values."

She pointed at the sign with its short quotes about why a title lands on this table. She did not read the quotes. She pointed the way a person points at a stain they want a clerk to remove. Her finger hovered an inch from the card that said Context is a tool, not a threat.

The crowd gave her a little circle of space. Some nodded. Some crossed their arms. Some checked their screens. People in small towns know how to let noise flow around them without losing their place in line.

I watched her while I kept half my attention on the door and half on the ledger cradle. Her tote bag hung on her left shoulder. It had the PTA logo silk-screened on it in teal. It bulged with flyers and a roll of tape, the narrow kind you use to fix a poster to a wall. A small water bottle stuck from the side pocket. Her phone lived in her right hand. The case was pink with a line of daisies along the edge. On her cardigan, a pin with the school's hawk. On her feet, white flats dusted with a veil of powdered sugar from brushing past Bria's table. No stains above the toes. No splash on the arch. No crumbs stuck in the seam near the heel.

Asa stepped back from the curb and let the air settle. He watches without writing when he can. He lets a person give the room the shape they think they own. He knows that shape pins them later.

"When did you last come inside," he asked her when she took a breath.

She turned to him, surprised to hear a question that simple. "I took photos of the table at eleven forty," she said. "I spoke to two mothers about resources. I stepped back out and stayed out because the alley was packed and I am not an EMT."

"That was before the collapse," he said.

"Of course," she said.

"What did you handle out here," he said.

"My flyers," she said. "The jar once for a wager about a teacher trivia question. The edge of the tent when the wind picked up. My phone. That is all."

Her tone wanted him to award points for grace under pressure. He did not grade. He asked the next thing.

"Do you have anything liquid or powdered in your tote," he said.

She looked down, then up, then forced a smile. "No," she said. "I have paper. Tape. A pen. Mints."

"Show me the pen," he said.

She reached into the tote and pulled out a slim fountain pen in a snap case. The barrel was resin in a pale blue. The nib was fine, steel, with a tiny scroll. She did not uncap it for him. He did not ask her to draw a line. He has been on sidewalks where ink becomes a scene. He knows when to keep a cap on.

"Blue or black," he said.

"Blue-black," she said. "It shades. It looks good on notes. I like it for thank you cards."

"Not gel," he said.

"Fountain," she said, a shade of pride under the word. "Greener, if you care about that."

He does care, but for a different reason. He nodded. "Keep it capped," he said, and moved his attention to her shoes.

He crouched without show, like a man tying his own laces. He looked at the sugar dust on the toes and at the clean edge near the sole. He did not touch. He stood again and glanced at the tent. Bria lifted a lid and tapped it twice to settle the plastic. The powdered sugar stood in a sunlit cloud above her table for a breath, then sank. People leaned back just far enough to save their shirts. I have seen some things like that turn into messes. Today the air carried the dust away without a fight.

"Where were you when the cup tipped," he said to Nina.

"Here," she said, and put her feet where she had likely put them at twelve fourteen. The mark of a heel showed in chalk near that spot. Rafi had dropped it when he set cones. He had not noted her mark on purpose. He had kept moving fast. It still gave us a rough place on the ground. She stood inside it now by reflex.

"Where was your tote," he said.

"Left shoulder," she said.

"Show me the inside," he said.

She blinked at that. "On camera," she said, with a little tilt toward Sylvie.

"On camera," he said. "Your choice."

She lifted the tote and pulled items with a care that wanted to be seen. Flyers. Roll of tape. A pencil case with a sharpener and two more fountain pens in different colors. A slim notebook with the school crest embossed on the cover. A small bottle of water half finished. A pack of breath mints. A makeup compact. A folded brochure from the church about today's bake. No bag of powder. No vial. No spare cups. No sticky note with the kind of half numbers and arrows that point to bad windows.

"Is that all," he said.

"Yes," she said.

"Thank you," he said.

She repacked as if he had rifled and she had to fix the mess. She set the pen case on top so the blue cap would show through the opening. She turned the tote so the logo faced the lens. She was not done speaking.

"You keep asking me about my bag," she said to Asa. "Ask her about that table," she said, and cut her chin toward the window again. "Ask why we need to celebrate material that tells young people their parents are the villain."

Paula came up the step then and placed herself in the space between the word celebrate and the glass. She had the ledger envelope in her hand with the note I had scrawled across the front. She did not hold it as a prop. She held it so the paper would not bend at the corner.

"The table is not a celebration," she said in a voice that holds classrooms and boardrooms without shouting. "It is an index. It places context where a loud person might remove it. If you pull context, you hand your kids the dark without a lamp."

Nina aimed her words at Sylvie's lens again. "Librarians do not get to make policy," she said. "Parents do."

"Policy lives in law," Paula said. "Not outside a shop on a day like this. You will not reroute money or meaning with a speech, no matter how sharp you make your vowels."

Sylvie did not nod or smile. She let the clip roll. She will cut later. She will text me the draft and I will send back a phrase that takes the heat out of the wrong parts and leaves a clear report on the day.

Rafi set one cone in the mouth of the alley and one near the curb. He gave a short wave to the juniors, who took the hint and slid toward the church side yard to give the paramedics a lane if they needed to return. He looked at Nina's shoes again. He has worked enough pastry tables to know the difference between dust from a bag and dust from a pass. Her toes held a film where you expect it if a person has leaned into sugar to make a point. No clumps.

No streaks. No wipe marks on the sides where a person would have brushed off residue from a spill. The powder told a small story. She had been near the tent and nowhere else.

A mother stepped close and asked Nina for a flyer. Nina handed one over with a smile that played to the corner of the lens. Her pen case clicked as it hit the tote rim. The fine nib sat safely under the cap. No gel line glistened. No rollerball head peeked from a cup.

Asa let her talk into the camera for another minute, then thanked her and stepped to the right so someone else could ask a quieter question. He did not argue. He did not explain policy. He is careful with his voice when people want a stage. He saves the words that change paperwork for rooms that have fewer phones and more forms.

Martin drifted to the edge of the cluster and kept his mouth closed. That was rare. He looked at Sylvie's lens and then at Paula's envelope and did not like either. He stepped back to the jar and dropped a bill in without looking at the amount. The jar gave a deeper note.

"A pull would calm the room," Nina said, keeping her line alive. "We all want a calm room."

"Calm comes from truth," Paula said. "Truth comes from records and from care. You do not have the right to frame this on a table when a cup and a pen are doing the harm."

Nina flinched at pen, a quick tell for anyone watching her eyes. Then she caught herself and put her smile back on.

"Do you want a pull quote," she asked Sylvie, trying to grab the shape of the post.

Sylvie glanced at me. I gave a small shake of my head. She understands the difference between a quote a person hands you and a sentence that serves a town.

"Say what you want the board to hear," Sylvie said.

"We want the table removed by morning," Nina said. "We want a written protocol for how the shop informs parents. We want an advisory fund to make sure parent voices have the resources they need."

There it was again. Advisory fund. Same phrase that had shown up in black gel under the first line of my ledger. Her mouth had the muscle memory for that string of words. It did not make the gel line hers. It made the day's script look more like a plan and less like a string of moments.

Paula heard it and filed it in the part of her brain that keeps minutes and motions. Her stare did not move from Nina's face. She could date a policy by a noun.

"You will get your time on the agenda," Paula said. "You will not get the money you tried to peel off a ledger with a phrase."

Nina's eyes flashed. She had not expected the word peel on a public strip. She masked it with a scoff. She tossed a line to the crowd about transparency. She said the shop should have told parents in writing that this display would be here. She said a table like this brings in strangers who watch our children without permission. She let that line hang like smoke and waited for fear to rise. It did not. This was a bake day. People know each other here. We can see who belongs by the way their hands hold a plate.

A father with a stroller asked if the jar was still matching. Rafi said yes. The father put in five and told his toddler they had helped buy books. The toddler clapped. The clapping made a better sound than the jar.

Sylvie took a breath and closed her clip. She did not hand Nina the shape she wanted. She turned slightly and asked Paula for one sentence about restricted gifts. Paula gave it, clean and narrow. Sylvie asked me for a sentence about shop policy on event displays. I gave it, short and boring. She knows short and boring keeps rooms from catching fire.

Asa stepped aside and let two neighbors pass to the tent for a refill. He watched the urn, the tray, and the set of cups in the crate. He watched Bria's hands go from lid to tong to bag. He watched Martin not watch the ledger. He watched Nina pull her tote closer and check her phone for comments. He keeps his eyes on the three places that move money and time.

"Tell me about the timer," Nina said suddenly, to me, not to Sylvie. "Why did the lights go out at the club last month. Why are you always playing with this stuff. It makes people uneasy."

"Wrong day," I said. "Wrong room. Wrong target."

She pushed the point for two more questions. I let them fall. I will not give her free rent in my head when a page needs guarding and a chain needs tying.

Let me be plain about one thing. Nina had noise and a motive you can sell in a feed. She did not have hands on the objects that matter. She did not touch cups. She did not step near the bar. She did not uncork a bottle or tear a packet or wipe a rim. Powder on her shoes told you where she stood. The tote told you what she carried. The pen in her case told you what kind of ink she favored. None of it fit the cup in my sleeve or the gel line that tried to reroute money through a phrase.

That does not make her harmless. That makes her useful to the person who wants a fog around the alley while they write a line in my book and smooth a sticker on a box. Loud people are perfect cover when quiet hands need ten seconds of room.

Sylvie leaned toward me as the cluster thinned and said, low, "I will post a clip. Neutral language. I will put the ledger sentence in the second slide with the blur on donor names. I will put your rule under it."

"What rule," I said, keeping my face blank for the nearby ears.

"Context stays," she said. "Funds honor their header."

"Fine," I said. "Add a line about patience, not panic."

"Done," she said. "Do you want a draft first."

"Post it," I said. "I will send you a correction if you miss a noun."

She smiled. She knows I like my nouns pinned to boards and not left to wander.

She moved three steps, thumbed her screen, and let the clip fly. The caption read what we had said. The second frame held a tight crop of the ledger line with the phrase Parent Advisory Fund. The donor names above were out of frame. The sticky note that read Held for review glowed like a lighthouse in the top right. Under that, the simple sentence, Restricted gifts are not a pickpocket. Under that, one more line, The shop remains open. No net. No speech. No flame.

In the comments, the town did what towns do. Some praised the bake. Some worried about Harold. Some cheered the table. Some shouted at the table. Some shouted at the shouting. Nina's account threw a block of text at the thread. It landed heavy. Then it sank. You can hear when a sentence does not stick. It makes a dull sound.

A woman with a toddler on her hip came up to Nina and said, kind, "We disagree on this. I still want you at the book fair next month." Nina said she would not be replaced so easily. The woman nodded as if to say, no one said replaced. You can learn a lot about someone's fear from the sentence they choose when no one is accusing them.

Asa gave me a look that meant, ready. We went inside, past the line where the jar lives, past the banned table where Peppermint had decided to monitor a copy of a novel about a girl who learns to listen to herself. I put my palm near his ear so he would not fling his paw at the ledger cradle on a whim. He blinked, then settled his chin on the cover as if to claim jurisdiction over fiction. Cats like to pretend all nouns report to them.

Inside, the counter felt like a dock. The ledger sat in its cradle with the mylar sheet secured, the neon sticky bright, the slip with my note taped at the edge. The gel line had not moved. Of course it had not. Ink does not grow feet. People give it those. We had time to roll the camera back and find the hand.

Before we did that, I took one more look out the window. Nina had shifted to a knot of parents and was handing out flyers from the top of her tote. Her smile rested on her teeth like a glove. The blue fountain pen sat on the tote's rim, cap on. Powder still dusted the toes of her white flats. No new marks. No new story. She would go home and write a long post about the sanctity of childhood and the danger of tables. She would hit publish. It would gather likes from the same dozen accounts that like everything she writes on this topic. It would not put a drop in a cup or a line in a book. It would, however, give the town an easy villain to argue with while the real work happened under good light in rooms that smell like paper.

Sylvie's post pinged my screen. Two frames. Clean captions. A thumbnail of Nina pointing at the sign, eyes lit. Under it, a one line summary that anyone could read without getting pulled into team jerseys. The clip made Nina look like motive without making her look like a hand. That is the difference between a piece you can use in court and a thing you share to watch comments burn.

Useful misdirection, I wrote on a card and slid it under the register tray where only my fingers go. Then I pulled the camera feed and rolled to twelve twenty. If noise is a fog, cameras are a wind. We let it blow.

CHAPTER 6

Flour Trail

The stockroom is where the shop tells the truth. Out front we make displays and tidy faces. Back here, the floor knows who dragged what where and when. The light is flat, the concrete holds every footprint a day leaves, and the metal rack by the back door carries our canvas totes like a small army waiting for orders.

Rafi and I pushed through the swinging door and let it breathe shut behind us. The hum of the fridge settled under the sound of the alley. Far off, the church bell gave a short quarter note and stopped. I took that as a small grant of time.

"Inventory first," I said.

"Roster," he said, already at the clipboard that hangs from the peg above the tote rack.

We run these events on habit and paper. Each tote has a number stenciled near the handle in faded blue. The event roster lists who checked which tote out and what it carried. It is not pretty, but it is ours, and it keeps people from wandering off with a bag full of napkins and our only good tongs.

Tote 1 through 4 went to the tent. Tote 5 lives at the espresso bar with sleeves and lids. Tote 6 holds paper towels and cleaner for spills. Tote 7 is the odd one, the ferry between front and back when we run short of cups. Tote 8 is the donation jar's emergency change before we seed it. Tote 9 is a mystery bag that never seems to hold what its list says it should. Today it was supposed to hold extra tablecloths. Today it did not.

I ran a hand along the handles and felt grit. Not the fine grit of cardboard dust, but something softer, a coat that wants to live on fingers. I pulled Tote 7 forward with two fingers at the very top seam and set it on the table we use to sort arrivals. The canvas sighed as it settled.

"Wait," Rafi said, and reached for the gloves.

We do this by the book when the day turns certain kinds of sharp. He pulled a box of nitrile from the shelf, popped the lid, and held them open so I could slide in. He put on his own pair and set a clean sheet of freezer paper on the table under the tote. The paper tears clean and gives you a bright background for photos. He clicked the task lamp a notch brighter so I would not have to fight shadows.

The tote looked like every other from five steps away. Close up, the bottom seam wore a faint pale haze that the others did not. I leaned in. The grit along the hem came away on my thumb as a fine white line.

"Flour," I said.

Rafi put his face near the edge and took a careful sniff. He has a good nose for ingredients. "All-purpose," he said. "Plain, not cake flour. There is a hint of lemon on it from the tent air, but that could be me."

He pulled the roster and ran his finger down to Tote 7. Today's box held a line that said "stash at front, overflow cups," and his initials. The out time was 9:14. No return time yet. The note column said "never left the shop."

"Tote 7 should not smell like a bakery," I said.

"And it should not look like it rolled in a sack," he said.

I crouched to look at the bottom edge where a tote kisses floor. The seam wore a thin pencil line of grime, nothing new. Next to it, at the back right corner, a short smear of something dark sat on the canvas like a fingerprint from a gate. Not round, not a circle, more of an arc with a tooth at one end. I had seen that tooth shape already today.

"Gate bite," I said.

Rafi nodded. "Lower hinge," he said. "The hinge tooth on our alley gate has that notch. I cut my knuckle on it last spring. Asa asked me to leave it so it could keep people honest."

We carry a small kit on the stock shelf because this is not our first bad noon. I took out the camera, set the ruler card beside the corner, and took a photo that gave me the smear, the hem, and the free edge of the freezer paper for contrast. Then a close photo of the flour dust on the hem where it had settled in the weave. Then one of the tote number stenciled near the handle. The dull paint had chipped at the top of the seven.

"Flour inside," I said, and opened the tote mouth with two fingers on the handles.

Rafi held the bag open so I could keep angles clean for the camera. I shot the interior before my shadow could tell a lie. The tote belly held a faint dust across the canvas that a person who had not spent years around bagged flour would call nothing. The county lab would call it residue. The strap ends wore it thicker, where they had brushed something powdered at hip height.

"Lids," Rafi said, reading the label on the inventory card clipped to the tote. "Overflow cups. Two sleeves of eight ounce. No lids listed."

I picked the sleeves up one at a time by the plastic wrap and set them aside. Under those, a roll of paper towels and a stack of napkins sat in a neat brick. Under that, nothing but canvas and dust and the kind of lint that comes with a life near paper. I smoothed the belly of the tote with a flat palm and watched the dust trail along the weave.

"Not tent-exposed dust," Rafi said. "Tent air settles on tops of things, not on the inside belly of a bag unless someone opened it near the flour table and set it down there."

We looked at each other. People set totes down when they need both hands. They set them down near their hips. They open a pocket with a finger and tuck a small thing away. They do not count dust patterns in the moment. Later, those patterns turn into sentences.

"Pocket check," I said.

Rafi pulled a small flashlight from the hook and trained it at the inside pocket near the seam. The pocket sags on Tote 7 when it sits too long. Today it held a small stiffness.

"Something is in there," he said.

I reached in with two fingers and felt a folded square of paper against the canvas. It was small and stiff and smooth, the kind of sticky note we stock near the register because people like to leave notes on cookbooks for friends. I pinched the top and drew it out onto the freezer paper. It left a faint rectangle on the canvas where it had pressed flour into a picture frame.

The square had been folded once and then folded again to make a small tab. Whoever did that did not want it waving in a pocket. They wanted it stiff and hidden. I set it down and looked for smudges with my flashlight before I touched it. Fingerprint dust is not a tool I carry because I do not like to pretend I am a lab, but you do not need a kit to see if a thumb left oil on bright paper. The square looked clean to my eye, which might mean gloves or clean fingers, or that the person had touched edges and not faces.

"Photo," I said, and took one from above with the note as it lay folded, then one at an angle that showed where it had sat in the pocket.

"Ready," Rafi said.

I eased the fold open. The paper whispered. Inside, a short line in a dark gel ink sat near the top edge. No greeting, no explanation, just a call time and an arrow.

12:20 → pour

The arrow was a simple line with a small sharp head. The word pour had the kind of o that people draw when they learned cursive and never unlearned it, round and soft. The p had a long tail and a flat top. The two in the time had a flat base and a small serif at the top like a hat pin. The colon sat even, not high. The line thickness told me a gel, not a ballpoint. We sell three gel brands that lay a line like that. Two of them are popular because they do not smear on glossy paper. The third is the one Rafi prefers to keep behind the counter for signing requests when someone wants a nice arch to their name. The stroke here sat with the same velvet look.

"Looks like our gel," Rafi said, voice bare of drama.

"It looks like our gel," I said, and took the photo that would make the comparison when the hour came. I placed the small proof ruler on the edge of the note so the lab would not have to guess the size later. I took one more shot closer, then one of the lineup with the tote number and the ruler card in frame.

"Who writes call times on a sticky," Rafi asked, more to the room than to me.

"People who do not trust their heads," I said. "People who like to make a plan look casual."

"People who work in rooms with schedules," he said. "Or people who learned to stage scenes for a living."

We both thought of Jenna with her tripod and her habit of turning noise into a living. We both filed it and did not let it turn into a verdict.

I slid the note into a small evidence sleeve, pressed the flap shut, and wrote the time, the place, and the tote number in the white block with a fine Sharpie. I write careful when paper starts pointing with arrows.

"Chain," Rafi said, handing me the log board. I put my initials next to the entry that read Tote 7 note, folded, ink gel, and the time. He initialed beneath. We keep the board because I have been in rooms where a defense attorney turns a missing scribble into a missing hour.

We bagged a small swab of the flour dust from the tote hem with a strip of tape and sealed that too. Lab work may tell us nothing more than the brand and the mill. It might tell us nothing at all. It still fits in the story.

"Bring the tote," I said. "We will set it on the mat by the back door and take a shot of the gate tooth for match."

We carried the tote back to the door and set it on the mat where stock meets alley. The air had shifted cooler. The tent music had gone quiet while someone retuned. The alley gate stood where we left it, open to the first chain link and latched so the lower hinge tooth presented itself like a tiny animal with a chip in its jaw.

I crouched and took a photo of the hinge. The tooth had a notch, not round, more of a bite shape, with one small flake of the old black paint lifting to show the rust beneath. I set the corner of the tote near it and brought the lens down so both smear and tooth sat in the same frame. The arc on the tote matched the angle on the gate. You could not call it a signature, but you could call it a handshake.

"Paint transfer," Rafi said, pointing at a small flake caught in the weave right at the arc.

"Bag it," I said.

He lifted the flake with the corner of a fresh tape square and sealed it in a second tiny sleeve.

"What is the chance this tote hit the gate in some past life," he said.

"Near zero," I said. "Tote 7 lives by the front. It goes to the bar and back. It has no call to flirt with the gate unless someone carried it to the alley. The roster says it never left the shop. The hem dust says otherwise."

He nodded. "And the pocket says a person made a note for a time window and did not want to carry that note in a palm," he said.

The back door frame wears a coat of green paint that refuses to settle. Along the inside edge near the latch, there is a smudge where a tote likes to kiss when someone squeezes through with more in their hands than they should. I put my face near the frame and saw a faint pale brush near that smudge. I held the tote up to the frame and watched the hem line up.

"Canvas touched here," I said. "Not long, not hard. Enough to leave a print if you know how to see it."

Asa's footsteps came up the back hall. He was talking to someone on the radio with a voice that said he had more rooms to corral and fewer hands than he wanted. He stopped when he saw the table, the gloves, the tote on the mat, the camera set to macro. He is quick. He reads a room like a cop. He reads my room like a clerk.

"What is it," he said.

"Tote 7," I said. "Roster says it did not leave the shop. Bottom seam says it met flour. Back right corner says it kissed the gate tooth. Inside pocket gave us this."

I held up the bagged note. He took it with the same care he gives to teacups and small lives. He read the line, twice.

"Twelve twenty arrow pour," he said. He turned the sleeve over and looked at the back in case a second sentence hid there. Nothing. He held it so the light told him the ink sheen.

"Gel," he said.

"Looks like our peg brands," I said. "We will pull sales when we get a breath. For now, the content."

"Call time," he said. "Not a private reminder like drink water. That is a cue."

He looked at the tote again. He crouched and ran a finger in the air along the hem without touching. "Dust inside," he said.

"Belly is powdered," I said. "Not thick. Enough to tell you someone opened it where flour lived a minute ago."

"Who carries Tote 7," he said, still crouched.

"Front of house," Rafi said. "Me or Liora. Sometimes a volunteer on event day when I point at a thing and forget to say please."

Asa stood and looked at the rack, the roster, and the tote number. He stepped past me to the door, reached out, and tapped the hinge tooth with a knuckle. It gave a small, patient sound. He looked back at the smear. He nodded.

"Good catch," he said. He does not waste adjectives when nouns do the work.

I glanced at the clock. The minute hand crawled toward half past. Out front, Paula would be filling a request for a quiet book with a happy ending for a child whose mother did not want to look at the alley while her hands shook. We had work here that would shape how the hour behaved. We pushed forward.

"Who knew where this tote lived," Asa said.

"Anyone who has ever looked behind the counter," Rafi said. "It hangs two steps from the mop. You do not hide a tote rack in a room this size."

"Who reached behind the counter today," Asa said.

"Me," I said. "Rafi. Paula. Bria when she grabbed gloves. Jenna twice when she asked if she could borrow tape. Nina hovered. Martin leaned."

"Leaned," Asa said, with a small tilt of his head toward the door where the ledger sits.

"Leaned," I said. "He put his elbow near the pen cup and his ring near the corner of the page. He did not touch the tote, not that I saw. The bar camera will show hands. The top camera will show the ledger slide."

"Jenna," Asa said. "Twice for tape."

"Both times I put the tape in her palm," Rafi said. "She did not fish for it."

"Good," Asa said. "Still, the alley gate tells me someone carried this to the back, past your line."

He took another look at the note, as if a small confession might grow on the paper if he willed it. It did not. Paper holds what you write and nothing more. He slid the sleeve into a larger bag with the tote number on it and sealed that. He set the tote itself on the table and tagged the handle.

"Keep the bag here," he said. "Do not let it travel on my desk. I will pick it up when I pull the gate camera. If the chain puts this bag in the alley while you were at the bar, I want that frame."

"Copy," I said, because sometimes a short answer keeps a room from spinning. He turned toward the door and paused when Peppermint's head poked under the swing like a stage cue.

"Do not let him go fishing," Asa said.

"I will not," I said. "He is not allowed to testify."

Peppermint stepped in as if he had known we were talking about him. He sniffed the tote base, sneezed once at the flour, and looked offended by a powder that did not smell like tuna. He circled the table, tested the freezer paper with a paw, and then hopped to the safe ledge we keep cat-free when we have to, because he thinks rules are challenges and I think they are bridges.

"Ask me what I want to ask," Asa said, gently.

"Ask it," I said.

"Could a volunteer have moved this without ringing you," he said.

"Yes," I said. "Paper needs a small oversight committee. Bags do not. A hand that belongs here could have walked in, grabbed the tote, stepped into the alley, brushed the hinge, set it down by the flour, picked up a cup, and reversed the route. Five minutes, two if you hustle."

He nodded. That kind of walk is a thing anyone who works events knows. Small tasks that break the chain because a person who sees a fix in reach grabs it.

"Or," he said, "a hand that does not belong here could have leaned, lifted, and pretended to belong."

"I did not see that hand," I said. "I was watching cups. That is not a defense. It is a fact."

He does not punish facts. He uses them.

We walked Tote 7 back to the rack. I set it on the shelf under its number and slid a bright sticky across the handle that read Hold with my initials and the time. I taped a second sticky to the rack upright so no helpful person would reshuffle bags.

"Pull the point of sale," Rafi said to himself, already moving to the register to check gel pen sales for yesterday and this morning. "If someone bought one with a romance paperback, the receipt will sing. If someone peeled one from the peg and pocketed it, the gap will still sing."

"Sing," I said. "I like that. Make the lineup. I want brand, SKU, time, and any card names for loyalty. If the ink on this note belongs to a pen I sold, the roster will help us hear whose song."

Peppermint flicked his tail. He has no patience for human metaphors when small toys exist. He pretended to attack the freezer paper corner and then resigned himself to watching the door like a sphinx.

I stepped out to the alley to look at the gate tooth again. Up close, the rust sat in a flake that begged fiddle fingers. Behind it, the weld looked strong and old. A smear of pale canvas dust now sat under the tooth from where the tote had kissed it, a small new halo that made the shape familiar. I took one more photo and made myself walk away.

"Back cam," I said to Rafi when I returned. "Give me a line from eleven fifty to twelve thirty. I want every frame where a tote element moves."

He nodded and set the monitor to split. The top left showed the bar. The top right showed the back hall. The bottom left gave me the door. The bottom right gave me the alley mouth cut by sun and shade. We rolled through until the club fell silent, stopped rolling when the hour broke, then eased frame by frame until a person brushed the rack with a hip. A hand slid along the canvas handles, then a shoulder carried weight.

We did not see a face. We saw a jacket in the corner of the frame in a neutral gray. We saw a wrist with a watch flat and black and thin. We saw a hand with no ring. We saw a body with a pace that did not speak panic. That body stepped through the back door and brushed the frame. The tote hem touched the green paint and left the faint line my eye had seen. The tote disappeared into the alley and back again a minute later, now a hair lower on the body like it held a cup inside or a small jug of something darker than water.

"That is a walk," Rafi said. "Not a run. A person who believes they are allowed to be here takes that pace."

"Or a person who knows how to be a shadow," I said.

We marked the time. We froze the frame with the hand on the tote. We printed two stills and wrote the clock on each. Then we did the most important part. We stepped away from the monitor so we would not start seeing words that the pixels did not write.

I slid the bagged note into the evidence box and closed the lid. The flap made a crisp sound. My hands felt clean. The room felt a little less so.

"Call time and an arrow," Rafi said, shaking his head as if a short line could be a magic trick that turned a street into a stage.

"Arrows point," I said. "They do not move your hand. Someone still has to pour."

He nodded and went to print the gel pen sales. I went to check the bar for hands. The jar sang once more as if to remind me that a community can hold more than one thing at a time. Somewhere across the tent, a child laughed at a joke about a cat who steals cake. Our cat blinked as if to say he would never, then looked at the tote handle like it owed him a game.

"Bag it," I said, to no one and to myself, and I did.

CHAPTER 7

Pen Match

The counter is where money and ink pretend to like each other. When I need answers fast, I start there. People think a register is a box that eats cash and spits change. Mine keeps a history. My drawer holds coins, paper bands, and a tidy stack of thermal tape that can prove where a hand stood at a moment most folks forget. Above it sits a peg rack with small luxuries. Page flags, lapel buttons, and a neat line of gel pens that make people write longer notes than they meant to. The rack looked innocent. I have learned not to trust innocent.

Rafi met me at the register with the master key and the look he gets when a hunt turns technical. We had bagged the sticky note from Tote 7 with its neat little "12:20 → pour." We had a smear on the tote that shook hands with the alley gate tooth. That arrow needed a pen. I wanted to know if mine sold it.

"First step," I said. "Floor model test. Same paper, same light. I want to see if our lines whisper the same way."

He pulled the clear bin that holds the testers. The bin smells faintly of solvent and dust because we keep it near the tape display. Inside sat three capped pens with "SAMPLE" written on a sliver of masking tape. One black, one blue-black, one purple because someone once asked for purple and then fell in love with it, which means I now carry it because I am weak for joy.

I set a sheet of our sticky notes on the counter on a patch I had wiped with a dry cloth. No lotion sheen, no sugar drift from the jar, no steam in reach. I slid on gloves because you never lose a print case by being fussy. Then I uncapped the black sample and let the tip rest on the note for a breath.

Gel ink needs a start to settle. If you press too soon, you get a circle dark as a pupil. If the pen has been idle a day, you get a faint air burp. This one made a clean bead and then drew a line as even as a ruler.

I wrote "line weight test" and lifted the pen. The stroke sat on the paper with a soft sheen you see in the first ten seconds. The downstroke on the L swelled at the base then tapered. The dot on the i rounded smooth. The whole string looked velvet, not scratchy. I took a photo, then wrote "control" and drew a simple arrow, then a small "p" with a flat top like the letter in pour on our folded note. I pressed the nib hard into the paper for one count to mimic a careless hand. The bead looked the same as the darker specks on the folded note's colon.

Rafi crouched and watched the angle of the light instead of the words. "That sheen," he said. "It falls to satin at six seconds and dead at ten. Same as the sticky from Tote 7. Same base."

I slid the sample aside and opened the bag with the note just enough to line the edge up near my control without sharing air. The arrowhead on the note had that small tight triangle our sample makes when you pull away with a quick flick. The crossbar of the two in "12:20" sat low, just like the personal quirk that pens coax out of people when ink starts to feel like a toy. Nothing conclusive yet. Familiar, though.

"Blue-black," I said.

I uncapped the second pen and ran the same lines. Blue-black lays a different shadow. It also lives more in fountain culture. The sticky from the tote was black. The blue-black gave me nothing new except a rule out. The purple is fun but pointless in a showdown where someone tried to hide in a crowd. I capped both and set them aside.

"Thermal," Rafi said, tapping the printer on the right. "Sales tell stories."

"Pull Saturday, twelve hours back," I said. "And yesterday after five. Gel pen SKUs. Pairs with paperbacks. Pair with coffee if you have the patience."

"I always have the patience for paper," he said. He slid the admin key into the lock and cleared the screen into manager mode. He does this like a piano player who knows which notes make a room sit up.

Peppermint jumped onto the romance table and arranged himself like a furry paperweight. He likes this part. He thinks receipts are toys that crinkle just for him. I gave him a look. He blinked like a judge and pretended to nap.

Rafi ran the sales report with a filter for Stationery, subfilter for Pens, subfilter for Gel. The tape spool clicked to life and rolled a thin ribbon that smelled a bit like warmed plastic. He tore the sheet and set it flat, left to right, instead of curling into a ribbon. He knows I hate fighting curls when a clock matters.

"Yesterday," he said, sliding the first strip toward me. "17:12. One gel, black. One romance paperback, mass market, 'Harbor of Second Chances.' Customer used loyalty. Paid with card. No note in the comments."

"Receipt number," I said, already reaching for a pen I could use without touching other evidence. He tapped the slip.

"#64083," he said. "Time stamped 5:12 p.m. Cashier Rafi."

"Buyer name," I said.

He pointed to the loyalty line. "Keene, Martin," he said. "Five points."

Heat rose in my face, slow then sharp. Not because I had a villain. Because the grid tightened. I tapped the line with the back of the pen. "Say it again," I said.

"Martin Keene bought a black gel with a romance paperback at five twelve," Rafi said. "He used his loyalty number."

I wrote it on a clean card in block caps. RECEIPT 64083. 17:12. GEL PEN, BLACK. MASS MARKET ROMANCE. LOYALTY: MARTIN KEENE. I set the card in a sleeve with the printed strip and sealed the top. I put the bag in the evidence box and wrote the time on my notebook. I do not trust memory when the room starts to hum.

"Any other gels," I said.

Rafi ran the tape for the rest of yesterday. One runner at nine when a grandmother bought two in purple for note-taking club. One at ten this morning when a teen used cash and no loyalty. One at eleven ten from a man who asked three questions about paper weight and then bought a fountain pen, which is not a gel but still a useful sale. None tagged to Martin.

"Only one tied to a romance yesterday," he said. "Only one tied to him at all."

"Look at basket," I said. "What else did he buy."

Rafi flipped to the full receipt image and read. "Gel pen, black. Paperback, 'Harbor of Second Chances.' That is the one with the lighthouse. You sold one to Paula's nephew last month. And a scone," he added, because he always notices pastry.

That last bit does not matter to an arrest. It matters to the day. People buy pens with sweets when they plan to write lists. They buy pens alone when they plan to write instructions.

"Pull the slip," I said.

He printed the whole receipt to full width and slid it into a page protector so the thermal would not fade in a week. He clipped a small copy, labeled it with the number, and taped it to the inside of a manila folder we keep for fast stacks. He is neat. That helps me be fast.

"Run this morning," I said. "Sales between eleven and twelve thirty. Gel pens. Note intimacy. Anyone buy a gel with tea to go."

He nodded and set the range. The tape spit numbers like a horse in a stall after rain. He walked his finger down the list.

"Eleven twenty," he said. "Teen with cash. Blue gel. No loyalty."

"Not our line," I said.

"Eleven forty-seven," he said. "Office supply shift. Two blue pens, ballpoint. That is for Rafi because he burned through them. My note says sorry."

"Forgiven," I said.

"Twelve oh three," he said. "Fountain pen cartridge. Paula. Black. She was restocking a case. She left her card."

"Harmless," I said.

"Twelve sixteen," he said. "Cups. Three sleeves. No pen."

"Twelve eighteen," he said. "Two gel pens, black, cash. The drawer shows mixed bills, no loyalty. Camera will show hands."

"Pull that," I said. "But the one that sings is yesterday's. Martin bought a gel in the window before an event. He came today to help the narrative, not the ledgers."

I uncapped the floor model again and wrote the time from the tote note in the same way it appears. The two twelves. The colon. The small "p" shape. I compared it to the bagged square through the mylar. Same ink family. Same line width. The gel we carry lays a 0.7 millimeter track. You can tell a 0.5 by its spiky skyline where the weave fights. You can tell a 1.0 by its wet tail. The line on the folded square sat like a 0.7 that had time to dry. That is our middle child. It is the one people buy without thinking because it feels easy.

I snapped photos. Sample feed. Note. Ruler. The glint falloff at six seconds. The dead flat at ten. I shot a short clip to show the change for the visual file that helps a jury understand why a line can be a brand without becoming a lab result.

Rafi slid the loyalty file on the register so we could see the name that matched the receipt. Martin's number sat, haloed by three small hearts from a time I wrote them on everyone's account during a drive to get kids into summer reading. That was a week I needed to believe in people more than usual. He has bought cookbooks and two history hardbacks and six romance paperbacks. He likes tidy covers with lighthouses. He buys in pairs when a donor event nears. He has never bought ink here before yesterday.

"Bag the sample sheet," I said. "Mark it as control. Keep the pen in the bin. We do not need to tape it to the counter yet."

He slid the sample sheet into a sleeve and labeled it "control lines, black gel, brand A, 0.7," then dated it. He put the sleeve behind the till in the proof slot where I keep clippings and contracts that do not want to get bent.

We turned to the peg where the gels live. The rack had a small gap in the black row. I count that row every morning because people steal black and purple in equal measure and I have learned that the pair signals different kinds of drama. The peg should have held ten. It held eight. We had sold one to the teen. We had sold one yesterday to Martin. That cleared the gap. No theft, no quiet peel today. We had a clean sale that lived on paper. That is the best kind of clue. It gets a door and a label and a signature.

"Bring Asa," I said.

Rafi tapped his radio for him and used the tone that means I am at the counter with something that has a name on it. Asa came in quick but not rushed. He had the kind of walk that says both "I am listening" and "I will not be boxed."

"Receipts," I said, and held up the bag with #64083 and the copy of the loyalty line. He did not reach for it yet. He looked at the bagged note. He looked at the control sheet. He looked at the peg with its two-hole gap. He looked at Rafi. He looked at me.

"Say what you have," he said.

"Yesterday at 17:12," I said. "Receipt #64083. Sale: one black gel, brand A. One mass-market romance. Buyer used loyalty. The name on the line is Martin Keene. That is Harold's spouse."

"Today," Rafi said, "two black gels sold at 12:18 to cash. Might be kids. Might be anyone. The teen at 11:20 bought blue. No other blacks sold with a card besides Martin's."

"We matched the line weight and sheen on the sticky to our brand with a control," I said. "0.7. Black. It behaves like our floor model in light and dry. The arrowhead has the same little shape this brand makes when you flick up."

"And we have a note from Tote 7 that says twelve twenty arrow pour," Rafi said. "That sat in a pocket that has flour inside even though the roster says Tote 7 never left the shop."

Asa nodded. "That is three steps," he said. "Brand familiarity. Sale to a person of interest. Note that uses the brand to aim a time."

He slid the bag down from my hand and looked at the receipt through the plastic. He checked the number, the time, the item lines, and that little loyalty line we keep because it makes our people feel seen. He read the name there.

"You verified this on the console," he said.

"Yes," Rafi said. "I can print the back-end log if you like."

"Do it," Asa said. "I want it for when someone says the customer could have used someone else's phone number."

Rafi pulled the admin screen and printed the loyalty validation. It showed the phone digits with three stars in the middle, as our system hides for privacy. It showed the date and tiny hearts I drew. He bagged that slip too.

Asa held the bagged receipt and the bagged note up at the same time, one in each hand. He is not theatrical. He is methodical. He let his eyes switch between them twice. He exhaled once.

"Good work," he said. "I will walk this to the office. It will ride pins until I talk to him with a recorder running."

"He will try to explain how a gel pen is not a crime," Rafi said.

"He will be right," Asa said. "And wrong."

I left Rafi with the drawer and went to the gel rack. The two holes in the black row looked larger now. I straightened the tags so the price read clean. Three ninety-nine. People love the way that feels like not much and writes like plenty.

Paula came in at my shoulder without startling me because she walks like an index card. "Do I need to stand at the counter again," she said.

"You need to drink water," I said. "And you need to look at this line."

She did, without touching, and read. I told her about the sale tied to Martin and the time stamp. Her face shifted a degree, quiet grief for her town tied to quiet satisfaction that paper holds.

"Wording matters," she said. "The note says pour. It does not say serve. It is the word a person uses when they plan action, not hospitality."

"Lawyer talk in an apron," I said.

"Habit," she said, and left me with a squeeze of my arm that I actually let land.

I felt Peppermint watching. He had changed positions to sit with forepaws aligned like a librarian ready to stamp. He looked at the bagged note. He looked at the gel rack. He looked at me. Then he yawned and closed his eyes because he knows that patience is how cats win and how clerks survive.

Rafi printed the condensed register log for yesterday evening and tucked it into the folder with the receipt. He initialed the corner. I added my initials and the date. It is small, all of it. Lines on paper. Holes in a peg. A number on a thermal strip that fades if you forget plastic sleeves. It builds a ladder, though. You can climb it without guessing. Guessing is a hobby. Ladders are work.

I caught myself wanting one more line on the case file. One more item that wins the argument before it is argued. That is greed. I pushed it down and did the next thing instead. I walked to the display and checked the gel rack again so I could write the peg count in the event notebook. Eight black. Seven blue-black. Five purple. One missing dust cap I would find under the counter when Peppermint loses interest in his seat.

Asa returned from the back with his face set to neutral. He does that when he has to wear two rooms at once. He put the bagged receipt into his case and then paused.

"What did he buy with the pen again," he said.

"A lighthouse romance," I said.

He made no sound. He looked at the window where the bunting tried to stay cheerful for the children, and then at the corner where the jar held coins for the literacy fund under a ledger that someone had tried to tilt. He looked back at me.

"That kind of cover next to that kind of ink," he said, soft. "People always think sentiment will shield them."

"It does not," I said. "Paper does."

He gave me a small nod. Then he stepped back to give three teenagers space to ask where the fantasy with the dragon librarian was. Rafi pointed them to the back shelf and told them the dragon has a job and pays rent. They laughed and the shop felt like my shop again for a breath.

I took the control sheet out and wrote one more comparison line. I pressed down at the start to make a bead the size I had seen on the sticky note at the colon. The bead matched. That is texture. A lab can talk about dye components and resins later. My job is to lay down the physical story that gets a warrant. I set the sheet back in the sleeve with a card that said "Control lines drawn by Wren at 13:02, same paper, same brand."

Paula returned with a legal pad and wrote a sentence I loved. "Shop to maintain independent paper chain; ledger frozen; note and receipt bagged; restricted funds protected." She wrote it in block letters with her archival pen, date at the top. She put it in a plastic sleeve and left it on my counter because sometimes a sentence in firm ink makes everyone breathe cleaner.

We worked the next ten minutes like a grocery line on a storm night. Cups, questions, books by the bag, a grandmother tearing up at a cookbook she used to own. The jar chimed a tick more.

The tent line shrank and grew like a tide.

Then the front door opened and Martin stepped in without flinching at the bell. He had taken his blazer off. He wore a light shirt that pretended it had not been handled by a dry cleaner less than an hour ago. His hair sat just so. His eyes took in the counter and the rack and the elbows and the faces. He did not look at me. He looked at the ledger cradle and then at the peg rack and then at my hands.

"Has the store calmed," he said. He said it like a man who expects the answer to be yes and the tone to be grateful.

"It is holding," I said.

He gave me a smile that tried to share ownership of that word. Then his gaze slipped up to the gel pens. It stayed there a beat, half a beat longer than a browse. He shifted his weight and put his hand in his pocket and then out again. Rafi saw the same slip and wrote it on his own private card in his head. Asa, two steps back, saw both ours and Martin's.

"We will need a statement from you later," Asa said. "Not here."

"Of course," Martin said. "I am happy to help."

I did not speak. I thought of the sticky note in its sleeve with that simple arrow. I thought of the receipt bag that said his name on the loyalty line and the time. I thought of the romance with the lighthouse and a gel pen in a neat basket. I thought of the gate tooth kissing the tote and the flour dust that sits where a hand does something it should not.

Rafi's printer rolled once for a half-page order. He tore the strip and set it under the counter away from Peppermint's paws. He and I have done this long enough to feel a shop's pulse under our feet the way a sailor reads a deck.

Martin lingered in a space that made no sense unless you knew he needed to read our faces. I did not give him any letters. I picked up a roll of sleeves and put them into the cup dispenser like the room were an ordinary Saturday. He left as if he had decided the air did not give him a script.

Asa watched him go, then laid his palm lightly on the counter. "Time to move the talk," he said. "You two hold this room."

"We will hold it," I said.

He left for the station. Paula followed with her pad. Rafi pulled a short stack of romance paperbacks forward to fill the gap from the one Martin had bought yesterday, then paused, then put it back. Leave your gaps. Let people read absence the way they read words.

The door sighed closed. The bell gave a clean note. Peppermint stretched one paw and allowed himself a slow blink at me as if to say, put it on the card. So I did. I wrote, "Gel sold with lighthouse, 17:12, #64083. Loyalty: Martin Keene. Note ink matches brand. Rack count confirms sale." I slid the card into the proof box and turned the key.

Outside, someone laughed. Inside, water hissed, sugar lifted, coins chimed. The room did its job. The paper did mine.

CHAPTER 8

Promo Grudge

The library workroom smells like paste, dust, and a promise to fix what can be fixed. I cut through the public stacks with a half wave at Mr. O'Malley in biographies, then slipped past the Employees Only sign Paula dislikes for how it bosses. A book truck loitered in the doorway, stacked two tiers high with mysteries in paper jackets, a strip of blue painter's tape across the top shelf that read RE-SHELF WHEN DRY. Someone had mended a torn spine and sent it here to finish hardening. The carts in this room all wear little messages like that, plain and bossy, so books don't wander off before glue decides to hold.

Paula stood at the long table by the far wall, shoulders square, hair pinned up with a pencil. She had a book open on blocks, hinges up, a narrow spatula in one hand, and an archival brush in the other. Her expression landed between focus and the kind of anger that powers clean work. A phone buzzed, she ignored it. A clock ticked, she ignored that too. The room hummed with machines that live to keep records safe. A laminator winked. Two label printers blinked in sequence like patient traffic lights. The date stampers slept in their shallow drawer.

"This is not a good day for powder talk on a sidewalk," she said without looking up. "If I hear one more speech about protecting children from punctuation, I am going to tape a comma over someone's mouth and call it a kindness."

"Good morning to you too," I said.

She lifted the spatula and slid it under the loose hinge paper with the kind of confidence that makes an old book breathe easier. "Take a stool," she said. "Tell me you have clean chain on that cup before I read three thousand words of comments."

"We have the cup," I said. "We have the tote and a note. We have gel ink where gel should not be. I came for you because donors and ledgers live in your head." I glanced at the hinge. "And because you do not miss when someone tries to move words after a collapse."

She eased the hinge paper up, brushed a thin line of paste, and set it back with a kiss of the brush. "Ledgers hate drama," she said. "They like clean lines and dated hands. Drama steals ink. So. Speak."

I gave her the short chain. The tent. The stagger. The cup that wore crazing like a fingerprint. The tote that claimed it had stayed home and then betrayed itself with flour dust and a gate bite. The sticky note folded twice and tucked into the pocket, the arrow, the time. The gel sale tied to Martin's loyalty number the night before. The add-on line in my donation ledger in neat black gel that moved money under a phrase he keeps on his tongue. She did not interrupt. Her hands worked. The book sat calm as she pressed the paper down with a small bone folder. She handed me the bone while she reached for a paper towel. I held it and waited for the first verdict.

"You look for poison and lies," she said. "I watch for small thefts dressed as policy. We live in the same fight."

She reached into her tool tray and clicked the cap off a black pen. I watched the tip without thinking. Pigment, not dye. Fine felt point. Micron barrel, black with white print, a number near the clip. She touched it to a scrap strip to wake the ink, then wrote a date in neat block letters on the inner hinge where a future Paula will bless this repair. The line sat dense and flat, no sheen, no soft halo. It sank into the paper grain like ink that knows how to grow old without eating the page.

"You will ask what pens I carry," she said. "Archival only. Pigment only. Acid-free. I buy them by the box and guard them like salt. Fountain for edits in my own notes, never on anything that lives here. Gel is for holiday cards and children who like to watch ink glide. Not for records."

"I am asking," I said. "Not because I don't trust your hand. Because the room slides your name into comment threads every time someone fires up a rumor."

She pursed her mouth. "Rumor today says I am bitter, so I must want to pull down a donor," she said. "Rumor today says I hate the new hire, so I must want someone to bleed. Rumor today eats time. Fine. Look in my bag."

She set the pen down next to three others on the tray. Black, black, black. All labeled archival. She pointed her chin at her satchel. I pulled it closer and opened the flap as if it were a drawer in my own office. Papers in folders, a small roll of linen tape, two notebooks with tabs, a pencil case with two mechanical pencils and a fountain pen with a converter, a zip pouch with a travel brush and spare tips. No gel. No loose sticks in bright packaging, no bubble cap. I lifted the zip pouch and she nodded, so I opened that too. Spare Micron pens, a small eraser, a pair of tweezers that could grab a cat hair without breaking the paper under it.

"If it helps, write it on a card," she said. "Paula carries pens that do not smear on labels. Paula does not buy gel in your shop. Paula does not like jars."

"I will write it," I said. "I believed it before I looked."

She swiveled the book and pressed the hinge for a count of ten. "The promotion," she said. "Get it on the record."

"Your call," I said. "We can talk about that or we can not. It sits in the air anyway."

Her laugh had no joy in it. "This room works because we tell the truth to things that cannot lie," she said. "So here it is. I have twelve years here. I keep open hours, I keep minutes, I keep the place masks and signs away from a fight. The board hired an out-of-town face with a fed grant on her resume. She interviews like a daydream. She talks about synergy and growth. She will do fine if no one asks her to check the spine of an atlas under a heat lamp."

"Name," I said.

"Meredith Lowell," she said. "Came with a letter from a senator and a lab for her talk on media literacy. I will not knock the letter or the lab. We need money and we need someone who can move a room with slides. But the job is more than slides. It is fines and records and making sure Mr. O'Malley gets to keep forgetting his password without losing his card. They overlooked that part. See, there, I used that word and I hate how it sounds. The promotion went to a resume. The work stays on my table."

She put a palm on the book like she could read heartbeat through cloth. Her mouth softened. "I am angry," she said. "Yes. The kind that leans long, not the kind that hits a wall. Angry enough to leave some days, not enough to abandon my ledger. Angry at a board that thunked a stamp on a choice and clapped for themselves. Not angry at your table or your display. I like your little quotes. I like the way you teach context without turning into a sermon."

"So, no cup magic, no bonus lines in my book," I said.

"No cup magic," she said. "I poured nothing. I poured tea once for Miss O'Grady in nineteen eighty-nine and burned my thumb. I make coffee at home now. The only line I added this week lived on a mending slip for a travel guide. No ledger edits. No gel skates."

Her pen lay on the tray, ink tip safe from lint. I looked at it again. No sheen. My eye had learned that lesson this morning. "I wanted to hear it from you in this room," I said.

"You have it," she said. "Now what do you need."

She put the mended book aside and turned to a file drawer without waiting for my answer, because she already knew I had a question with the word Keene in it. Her hands found the right folder with the ease of muscle memory. She slid it out and put it on the table, then set a blotter sheet beside it for reasons only she knows. She does not let ink wake outside a blotter zone.

"Older issue lives here," she said. "Before we talk about poisons and cups, you need to see how money tries to herd narratives in this town."

She opened the folder and pulled a stack of minutes. The board meets twice a month and fills a lot of paper for very little action. She has every page labeled with a location and a date. She does not need the labels. She uses them to train whoever comes next. She laid out two years' worth of notes, then tapped a line that sat halfway down one page.

"Here," she said. "Two summers ago, a Keene donation for the branch refresh. Gift came with strings. Naming rights on the reading corner and a plaque with language pulled by their board. It read Families deserve shelves that reflect our values. The word values sparked a fight row to row. People hear values and some hear doors closing."

"What settled it," I said.

"Me," she said. "And an email where I swapped that word for choices and got Martin to sign off. He likes choices when he wants to look generous. He likes values when he wants to lock a room. He called me that night to say I had a way with tone. I wanted to say tone is a lever people use when they want to make other hands move. Instead I said thank you and wrote down the exact phrase for a day like this."

She slid a printout across the table. A photo from a ribbon event that year. Martin at a podium, Harold beside him, a board behind them with a header. Advisory Fund. The same phrase I had seen under my ledger line, the same phrase Nina loved on a sidewalk, the phrase that makes a gift look like a committee.

"Advisory Fund," I read. "Keeps showing up."

"They used it to move money into a pool they could steer," she said. "Not illegal. Ugly. Silent. The board put it up because who says no to cash when your roof leaks. I recorded the vote. I underlined the phrase in my copy. I put a tab on it and I have been waiting for the day a ledger somewhere else grew that line without a meeting."

"And here we are," I said.

"Here we are," she said. "You show me your ledger page and I will point at the curve in the r on the word advisory and tell you if it matches Martin's hand. I know how his fingers settle. He makes a neat r with a short leg, like he thinks speed is grace. He switches pens at odd times. Today he touched gel. He prefers a rollerball when he signs checks because the pen weight tells him he is important. If he wrote in your book with a gel, he did it in a hurry while he thought of three other moves."

"You do not like him," I said.

"I do not like money that arrives with a script," she said. "He can be charming. He can also sit at a table and smile while he folds a sentence around someone else's throat. Harold, to be fair, read books. He could sit with a story and keep his mouth shut until he finished a chapter. I am not speaking ill of the dead. I am speaking plain."

She turned a page and pointed at an entry from eight months ago. "Board discussed parental advisory signage. Martin proposed a set of talking points for clubs and events. He used the phrase protect without define. He moved a motion to add a line about parents in charge. That line failed. It failed because donors should not write policy dressed as common sense."

"Your minutes carry more fight than people expect," I said.

"Those pages keep the town from telling itself a false story later," she said. "I lose promotions to people who talk about brand sunsets. I win on days where someone needs to know who moved which noun and why."

Her phone buzzed. She turned it face down without looking. "Nina will want me to come outside and support a pull," she said. "She will say I owe the children my courage. She will say what she says until the comments tire of hearing her name. I will not come outside. I will stay in here and fix a hinge and then help you box a cup."

"Did you see the display this morning," I asked. "Before you came in."

"I walked through with a cart of returns," she said. "I read your placards. I read two of the quotes out loud under my breath to hear how the words held. I watched a grandfather explain a cover to a kid without making a speech. I saw a mother frown and then take a photo so she could fight with her sister about it later. That is what we do. We let speech breathe without shoving it into a bag."

She reached for her pen again, not gel, and wrote a note on a card. "Restricted means restricted," she wrote. "Add-on lines belong in meetings, not in panic. Staff will not move donor lines during a med call."

"That last sentence is very you," I said.

"Send it to your feed if you need a clip that replaces noise with simple," she said. "We both know half a town runs on screenshots."

She capped the pen and slid it into the tray. I looked into her bag once more, not because I doubted her, but because the habit keeps the room honest. No gel tucked in a pocket, no stray stick. Pigment pens, brush, clips, tape, notebooks, a wrapped granola bar she will forget until six. She keeps a system in there that runs on order, not on impulse.

"Tell me your supervisor's name again," I said.

"Meredith," she said. "We will do fine when she learns this room. She will throw up the first time glue lifts under her nail. She might start to understand where policy lives when a book falls apart in her hands."

"Will she back the table," I said.

"She wants donors to love her," Paula said. "She wants parents to stop sending paragraphs. She wants to write a grant about civil speech. She will float above the fight if she can. I will hold the floor for the staff who cannot float."

The laminator beeped. She pulled a fresh laminate from the tray, set it on the blotter, and trimmed edges clean with a metal ruler and a careful swipe. The lines sat perfect. The thing would not curl. She signed the back with her initials, date, and a note for which shelf will host it.

"What did you want to flag besides the old donation," I asked. "Anything else I should never miss from that file."

She smiled at the way I landed on that word. "Language drift," she said. "Watch for little shifts that try to move a policy while pretending nothing shifted. Two months ago the board minutes used briefer, then the chair said braver in a follow up when she wrote about a kids' panel. Braver is catnip for Nina. The shift looked small, but it invited a crowd to think programming equals courage. Courage equals fights. Fights equal clicks. Words matter when they hold tiny hooks under them."

"Noted," I said.

"And this," she added, flipping to a stapled memo. "Martin's email pushing an Advisory Fund talk for a donor breakfast. Look at the logo on the header."

I looked. A stylized book with three waves under it and a lighthouse, the current brand for the Keene Family Trust. A small detail sat in the corner, a tagline in light gray. Stories shape futures. I filed it in my head next to the civic version of the phrase. He wanted shape and story. He wanted to pretend fences help stories grow. He likes to borrow librarian words and fit them to his budget.

"He will try to frame today as a story about risk," she said. "Risk talks have a way of draining shelves. Fight him with records, not speeches."

"You are here because you know how to do that," I said.

She set the memo aside and rested her palms on the table. "Now ask me if I hate Harold," she said. "If I wanted him dead because he liked the advisory phrase. Ask me if I believe a post about context would murder a donor."

I sighed. "I already know your answer."

"Say it for the room," she said.

"You do not kill donors in alleys over a table," I said. "You do not lace a cup to spite a spouse who changes a plaque. You do not move money in a ledger while a man is down and call it a fund, not if you can help yourself. You also do not stand still when a hand edits a book after it falls to the floor."

"Good," she said. "Tape that to your cork if you need a credo."

She cleaned the brush, set it bristles up, and turned the book on its cradle so the cloth could cure without movement. She checked the edges with a fingertip, satisfied that they would hold. She washed her hands at the deep sink and dried them with a towel that had seen better days. She is strict about paper and easy on towels. It makes sense in a world that pays librarians less than donors think.

"While we are here," she said, "show me the add-on line. Not the whole page. I do not need names."

I slid the sleeve from my bag and put the ledger copy on the blotter. She leaned in, eyes sharp. She has a face that reads fonts before the rest of us read words. She studied the letter shapes, the way the pen met the paper, how the ink spread in the fibers. She hummed once and shook her head.

"Not Rafi," she said. "Not you. The hand sits higher in the wrist. The r looks like what I said. The i shows a short dot placed with speed, a flick, not a lift and press. The tail on the y looks like a stick with a foot, not a loop. It matches signatures in this folder. Someone had a script in a pocket and thought a panic gave permission to write it."

"Thank you," I said.

She put the copy back in the sleeve and tapped it twice, a private habit, superstition for luck. "You have your motive. He hides narrative with money. Your evidence will live in the pen and on a coat liner. My job is to make sure no one uses my job to hide blood."

"You hate the PTA drama," I said, because the scene list wanted that line and because it fit anyway.

"I hate television staged on a sidewalk," she said. "Bring your arguments to a table and write them down. I will host you with water and a timer. I will not clap for a woman who waves her tote like a sword and pretends the town handed it to her."

She picked up her archival pen and wrote a line in her notebook. I looked out the narrow window over the roof and saw clouds building where blue had promised to stay. Peppermint would be in my front window warming his belly without shame. He loves a window even on hard days.

"You will come for the Q and A if we hold one," I said.

"I will bring my pen and a page with definitions for restricted and designated," she said. "I will talk twice. Then I will sit down and let someone else talk. Librarians do not fix rooms by talking for an hour."

"Fix them how," I said.

"By showing people where records live," she said. "By holding steady when a rich man pouts."

She checked the time, then switched off the laminator. The light died. The room exhaled. Rafi texted me three words. Cleaner bag secured. I told Paula. She nodded once and underlined a date on a memo as if to say, see, this is where the fight started, not today.

I stood. "I am going to box the cup and walk the receipt to Asa," I said. "Then I am going to sell a multi to a woman who needs recipes that do not break her budget."

"Give her the cheap beans sheet," Paula said. "And tell her to read the chapter on onions in that cookbook you hate and I love."

"I do not hate it," I said. "I hate the tone. The advice stands."

She smiled, a thin line that softened at one corner. She picked up her pen and turned back to the mended book. "Before you go," she said, "write down this older issue in your file. Keene money arrives with phrases. Advisory fund is not a mole that crawled into your ledger by chance. The phrase lives in their boardroom. Today it tried to live in yours. Pull it by the root."

"I will," I said.

"Good," she said. "Now go. I am going to sit with this hinge until it holds."

She did not look up as I left. She did not need to. The book under her hands was halfway to whole, and her pen lay where it should, the tip ready to write the next date on the next repair. The workroom door sighed as it closed. Out in the stacks, the air smelled like dust and paper, the honest kind. I wrote a card for my pocket while I walked past travel and into reference. Paula supports the display. Paula hates the PTA circus. Paula uses archival black, no gel. Paula flagged an old Keene plaque and a phrase that will matter. Older issue in play. I tucked the card beside my phone and went back to a shop that had learned, again, how halls and counters hold a town together.

CHAPTER 9

Pastry Alibi

The bake tent ran like a small fairground. String lights, burlap runners, pie stands on risers, and the sugar drift that coats every surface by noon. People moved in loops from Bria's table to the brownies to the coffee urns, then back for seconds if a child asked nice. The talk sat on top of a hush that happens when a crowd has seen a man fall. You could feel everyone trying to be normal without breaking the hour.

Bria Leduc had flour on her sleeve and a Square reader in her hand. She stood behind her chalkboard sign, BRIA'S FAVORITES, lemon bars and coconut macaroons spelled neat with little stars. Her hair was tied in a scarf that matched her apron. The apron hid a tremor in her shoulders. She saw me, then saw Asa two steps behind me, and pulled herself straight.

"I did not pour anything," she said. No hello, no small talk.

"I know," I said. "We are going to show that with paper and pictures. Walk me through your sales at twelve twenty."

She glanced at the Square reader like it might save her. "We were slammed from twelve ten to twelve twenty-five," she said. "Lemon bars went first. I do not move from this spot when it is that busy. I have both hands full. My mother raised me to keep lids closed until a sale happens, so no one grabs with sticky fingers and no one sneezes on the tray. I stick to that."

"Good," Asa said. "Let us see your log."

She swiped to the history screen and turned the device so we could see. The tent Wi-Fi has a silly name, CATNIP_GUEST. Bria's Square pulls time from the network, so the stamps hold. The list showed a run of payments, short lines of item names and amounts, each with a minute and a second.

12:19:31 Lemon bar, cash.

12:19:58 Macaroons, card.

12:20:12 Lemon bar, card.

12:20:21 Lemon bar, cash.

12:20:44 Coconut duo, card.

The beats were tight, no gaps wide enough for a long errand to the tea tray. Each payment included the last four digits of a card or the word cash. Her device recorded item taps and tips in the way that tells you if a hand had time to wander. It did not. She was moving product, not staging anything.

"Scroll a hair up," I said.

She did. The top of the burst showed 12:18:54, macaroons, card, two items, a tip, an emoji the buyer added because teenagers like buttons. She had no voids, no stops, no half rings parked between items. I took a photo of the list, then had her tap the detailed view for 12:20:12. The screen showed the entry, the item, the tent tax, the small green check that means the network said yes. I framed the photo with the time, the item, and her gloved hand. She wore gloves, not because the county asks for them at bake tents, but because Bria likes rules and hygiene when sweets meet air.

"Match the pour," Asa said to me. He had his notebook open to a time grid. He had written 12:20 arrow pour from the tote note, then two lines for what we could prove on either side. We needed to put Bria inside her sales and out of the alley line at that second.

"Front camera," I said. "Sylvie filmed a sweep right then for her post. We can use it if she gives me the raw."

"Already asked," Asa said. "She is on her way with the card. In the meantime, what can we show here."

"The lids," Bria said, and set the reader down to lift a corner on a tray, then stopped herself with a look at Asa.

"Do it," he said. "Slow."

Bria snapped a photo of her own trays every time she closed them. She keeps a binder of ribbons and proof of presentation for contests. She pulled her phone from the apron pocket and opened her album. At 11:58, three shots showed lemon bars in neat rows, covered with a clear lid that fogged a touch at the corners. At 12:05, another shot showed a hand with a tongs lifting a bar, the lid balanced open on its hinge. At 12:20, the album showed a picture of a toddler with a cupcake two tents away that she had taken for his mother, then two pictures later a return to her station at 12:22 with the lid still closed on the coconut tray, condensation intact. The lemon lid sat open in that frame, but the hinge position matched a sale in progress. She kept a habit of resting a lid at a certain angle so it would not slam.

"Your trays at twenty," I said.

"Closed on coconut. Lemon open because I was serving. I can tell by the hinge and the light streak on the lid," she said. She has a baker's eye. She knows how plastic catches sun in a pattern that repeats, and that matters when you need to prove a stop never happened.

I walked behind her table and knelt to eye level with the lids. A fine pearled fog sat on the coconut dome at the top edge, a clear sign the lid had not been lifted in the last five minutes. If someone had popped it at twelve twenty to slip a cup in or out, that fog would have broken in little drips and cleared faster across the seam. The lemon dome had the expected handprint smudge on the top from where she uses the same touch every time she lifts. The smudge had sat long enough to attract a bit of powdered sugar. A fresh lift would have made a clean oval instead. I had handled enough catering lids to read them like a lab report.

"Leave them," I said. "We will photograph and let them be. Show me your cash box."

She opened the till and turned the bills to show they were wrapped neat by denomination with paper bands. Her mother's touch again. No change rolled loose where a hand could hide a packet. No odd scrap taped to the lid. I checked around the base of the table and found only a crate with extra napkins, a spray bottle of diluted vinegar for cleaning, and a small pack of wipes. No spare cups, no wedged saucers, no stray bag.

"You had both hands full," I said, not a question.

"Serve and tap. Serve and tap," she said. "If a person did not have cash, I set the tongs down to take the card and then picked them up again. I keep my elbows in. I do not reach past that chalk line," and she pointed to the tape line on the table edge that kept her board from drifting.

"Anyone reach your tray while your eyes were on the reader," Asa asked.

"Kids try to touch the coconut," she said. "Parents catch them. Adults behave. The only person who leaned in without asking was Harold when he wanted to see if I dust with more sugar now than last year. He brought his cup over to show me the color of his tea. We did that every year. He liked to see if I had changed."

"What time," I said.

"Before noon," she said. "Before they started speeches. He always came early to tease me, then came back with a plate to buy something he had already tasted once. He was loyal like that."

"After noon," Asa said, gentle.

"After noon I stayed here," she said. "He stopped by again at twelve sixteen when a woman asked where the lemon bars were from and he pointed at me and said my name like I was a vendor and a friend at the same time. He said he was going to make a speech about choices that would make Nina twitch. He laughed. And then he went for hot water. That is the last I saw him standing."

Rafi slid into my peripheral with a tablet he had borrowed from the espresso bar. He had synced the tent's camera to the shop Wi-Fi and pulled a clip. He set the screen next to the Square reader and tapped play. The clip came from a small dome camera we had mounted on the tent center pole for event nights. It watches for shoplifting and for safety if a child wanders. It had saved us once when a cooler tipped near a toddler. Today it gave us a sweep of the tables with a timestamp in the corner.

At 12:19:50 the frame showed Bria at her station with her left hand on the tongs and her right hand holding the Square reader. The camera caught the top of the reader and the back of the buyer's hand. At 12:20:12 Bria tilted the reader toward the buyer, who tapped a card or a phone. Bria clipped the tongs under her right thumb and handed over a bar with her left, then tucked the box back into its nest. She did not step away. She did not lift the coconut lid, and the lemon lid stayed open for the handoff, as expected. At 12:20:21 the cash sale popped on her Square log and the camera showed her bag a bar with both hands for a boy who could not decide if he wanted a corner. Both hands, both eyes down, exact work, no tea in reach.

That was the minute that mattered. I scrubbed the timeline forward to 12:20:44 and watched her accept another card with a nod, then tap out a thanks while someone behind her waved for more cups at the urn. She did not turn. She could not. You learn how a person works when the room asks for speed. Bria shrank her world to the span of her table and its lids.

"Alibi holds," Asa said. He said it like a person who knows the weight that lifts when you can say it out loud.

"Thank you," she said, and sagged an inch before she set her shoulders again. "Please keep saying it whenever anyone looks at me like I poured."

"I will," he said. "A camera and a log live better in a sentence than any speech."

"Tell me about your set," I said to keep us moving. "Where did your cups come from."

"We do not serve tea," she said. "We serve cookies and slices. The tent cups live by the urn. Those came from the PTA bulk purchase. I do not stock them. I did bring a spare stack of napkins. The cups that have a pattern on them are not mine, not the tent's. I saw one with a small hairline by the handle and thought it was one of your shop cups."

"It was," I said. "That hairline and the crazing pattern sent us to the sink. We have that cup and its partner saucer bagged now. Your lids tell me you did not set it down and pour. The urn area had three volunteers at noon. We will take their hands next."

She folded a wipe and pressed it flat without using it. People use their fingers when they need control. She needed to press something and chose a wipe because it would not hold oil. I liked how her brain worked.

"Who handled your cash while you served," I asked.

"My own hands," she said. "I leave the box against my hip. If a person insists on change while I am mid lift, I ask them to give me a second. No one else reaches in. It keeps the math clean and keeps gossip from turning into a theft joke later."

"Good," I said. "Your habits help you now."

She took the Square reader back and held it like a talisman. "If I had thought to take a picture at twelve twenty-one I would have," she said. "I only took that one at twelve twenty-two because the toddler with the cupcake grabbed my heart. His mother had both hands full with a stroller and a purse and a small person who wanted to show me frosting on his face. I never say no to a face like that."

"You did fine," I said.

Rafi reached under the table and picked up a lid to show Asa the hinge crank. "Look," he said. "Old style hinge, holds at ninety if you set it right. It falls at eighty. Bria's hinge sits at ninety when she serves. That is her tell. She has years of pictures that show the same angle. The lid did not hang midair because she already knows the trick. It either lay flat, or it sat upright."

"And the coconut lid stayed flat during the window," Asa said. "Condensation makes that prove itself. Good. We will film that for the file."

Bria set the lid down and gripped the edge of the table. She watched people drift in, then away, then back with questions about what would happen now. She is not a person who likes to be watched for the wrong reason. I do not either. You learn to hold your eyes quiet when an hour wants to tilt.

"Tell me one thing," I said, aiming for the small thread that would be our exit. "Yesterday. Tea schedules. Did anyone ask you when the urn would be hot or when the tent opened. Outside the usual chatter."

She nodded, then paused. "That man," she said. "Martin. Harold's spouse. He asked twice. First at the council hall after a committee check-in. He said, what time do you serve tea tomorrow, and I said we serve sweets, not tea, but the urn goes out at eleven forty-five. Then he came by here after four yesterday and bought a book with a lighthouse on it and a pen for a list. He stood where you are standing and asked again. It felt like he was pretending not to have heard. He wanted the exact minute for something. He said he had to time a speech. He did not need that for a speech."

"Exact words," Asa said.

"'What time does the tea go out,'" she said, and mimicked the tone without being cruel. "I said, the urn goes out at eleven forty-five, hot water starts to cycle just before noon, and it gets busy right then so you should pour early if you must. He smiled and said, early is smart, then left. That is the last time he spoke to me without a crowd."

Rafi and I shared a look. I wrote it on my card. Asked about tea times yesterday, twice. Phrasing matches his habit of steering with simple words.

"Thank you," Asa said. "You have been clear. Keep your station how it sits now for the next hour. Do not wipe the lids. Do not break the setup. We will take more photos and then you can feed a town again."

She gave a murmur that was almost a laugh and almost a sob. She breathed, pulled herself straight, and lifted her tongs. A woman stepped up with a wrinkled dollar and a request for the corner with extra sugar. Bria served her with care, then ran the card for the next buyer without letting her hands wander. At the edge of the table, a child reached for a macaroon and a parent caught the hand gently. The line moved. The tent inhaled and exhaled like a living thing.

I stood back with Asa and looked at the small cluster of facts we could name. Square log puts Bria at sales at the minute of the pour. Video shows her with both hands full at 12:20. Lids stayed sealed on the coconut until 12:22. No gap for a run to the urn with a single cup in hand. Her work posture never changed. That is the shape of an alibi. It will not comfort everyone on a sidewalk. It will comfort a jury that likes clocks.

"Trim her clean," Asa said, low. "If anyone asks, say it plain. She did not do it."

"I will say it plain," I said.

He tipped his head toward the alley where the urn crew stood in a knot around the hot water line. "We take them next," he said. "Then we visit a cleaner with a jacket that wants to confess."

Bria rang up another sale. Powdered sugar fell like tiny snow and settled on the table at the same angle as the sun. Peppermint slipped into the tent, decided the floor was sticky, and returned to his usual post. I filed the last line for this chapter on a card. Her log lives. Her lids hold. Her hands stayed on the work. Then I slid the card into my pocket and walked with Asa toward the steam.

CHAPTER 10

Teacup Glaze

The back sink gives me the kind of light that tells the truth. The task lamp over it is a flat white panel Rafi calls the noon-maker. It burns clean, no yellow, no romance, and it shows every stain a life leaves on ceramic. I snapped it to full and set a fresh towel on the drainboard. The cup sat on a metal tray beside a ruler card and three clean cotton swabs. Rafi had placed a folded tent ticket under the tray to keep it from ringing on the stainless. He does small kindnesses for the room without speaking.

Peppermint hopped onto the empty stool and thumped his tail once. He knows the sink is not for paws. He likes to audit.

"Asa wants the glaze story without poetry," Rafi said, passing me the loupe.

"Poetry is for the front table," I said. "Back here we talk glass."

Glaze is glass. Thin, poured, fired, full of secrets, and once it is crazed it wears those hairlines like fingerprints forever. You cannot force those lines to lie. People try. Vinegar baths, bleach, tricks with heat. Truth lives in the pattern.

I cradled the cup in my left hand and turned it under the panel until the sheen died and the hairlines came all at once. The interior looked clean at first glance. Then the web rose. Very fine, tight, like frost on a late window. The main starburst sat under the handle and ran to the lip in five spokes. Two crosshatches intersected on the north inner wall where a wrist would tap before a sip. I had seen that before.

"This is our stray," I said. "Espresso bar seat three, overflow cup. Rafi, you washed it yesterday at four."

He nodded. "And complained about the hairline on the handle," he said. "It catches the drying cloth. You said keep it for the sink, not the tent."

I set the cup on the towel and took the loupe to the handle. The hairline ran straight through the ear, a fine gray seam that looked like a pencil line under the glaze. It had a tiny chip at the top where the kiln gas had bitten a bubble. I found the chip months ago when a regular clinked it against a spoon hard enough to make me wince. It has lived with us long enough to belong to our inventory story.

"Photograph," I said.

Rafi leaned in and framed the handle, the hairline, and the chip with the ruler card. He clicked two shots, then took a third with the cup angled to catch the web.

I rolled the cup so the interior faced the panel. Under the loupe the crazing resolved into a map. The tight grid near the base plate was older, stained with the faintest brown that never fully lifts, even if you soak overnight. Higher up the lines ran thinner, newer. The stain line where the tea sat today showed a ring one notch above where the tent cups landed on every other pour. That told me the pour had been generous. It also told me the cup had seen stronger tea than the small styrofoam ones before. Foam cups do not hold heat the same way. Ceramic keeps it and paints it on the wall.

I rinsed the interior with hot water from the kettle Rafi keeps on the back stove and watched the meniscus marker fade a shade, then stop. Old tannin holds. New tannin lets go only so much. Where the tent cups from the PTA set had stained was lower, because they are smaller by a breath, and their curve is different. Our stray cup had a rounder belly and a narrower lip. If you pour the same volume into both, the line lands higher on ours. But the tent volunteers never pour the same volume. They pour to a habit. The line on the tent cups I checked sat a finger width down from the rim. The line in this cup sat half a finger at most. That is not a science unit. It is a shop unit that holds. When I listen, it talks.

"Measure," I said.

Rafi brought the calipers. We do not buy fancy, but we do buy what works. He held the inward lip and slid the jaw to the stain. Twenty two millimeters from rim to mark. Tent cups showed twenty six when we checked at the table. Our average pour in those during the rush hits mid twenties. Somebody filled this cup like a person who wanted a full show or a fast hit.

I turned the cup to read the foot. No brand mark, thrift store blank. The foot ring had a slight chip at one segment, a bite out of the clay that gives you a wobble if you set it on a glass counter. I felt that wobble two days ago when I put it down too fast by the espresso grinder and muttered at myself. It is in the bar log. Rafi writes petty griping in the margins. He thinks it amuses me. It does.

"Foot chip at seven o'clock," I said. "We log it on the first. It shows on the bar photo of the stray cup by the water station."

Rafi scrolled his phone, found the shot, and set it on the counter where I could see it next to the cup. Same chip, same shallow curve, same faint iron freckles in the clay along the foot. People think plain china matches if two whites sit close. You learn eyes. Our tent set is slightly blue. This cup sits warm against it. The panel made the difference scream.

I took a cotton swab and rolled it along the interior stain. The stick came away tan. I set it on the tray. I rolled a second swab across the rim where the lip meets glaze. It came away with the faintest bitter lift that had nothing to do with tannin. The on-the-spot strip we used earlier had already said yes to a bitter agent. I still check with nose. There is a smell you do not forget once you meet it. I capped the swab in a small tube and labeled it. Rafi dated and initialed. We keep chains closed.

"Look at the outer wall by the handle," I said. "See the tiny traction nicks."

He angled the panel. Tiny vertical scuffs lived in a little cluster where a right thumb likes to rest when a person lifts. Our bar crowd is mostly right handed. Those nicks are where rings kiss glaze. They sing on our stray cup. The tent cups show smooth walls, hardly anyone wearing rings while pouring batter for bake sales.

"Thumb nest," Rafi said.

"Thumb nest," I said, and took the shot.

I set the loupe down and worked the cup against a stack of tent cups we had pulled for comparison. Side by side the differences grew. Tent cup had a lighter foot, smoother bottom glaze, and the tiniest manufacturer's ghost under the foot from a stamp. Our stray had nothing clean under there, just raw clay and the chip we hated. Even the interior swirl at the base, where a glaze river freezes, sat different. Tent crock had a soft loop like a comma. Our stray has a slash.

"You said no poetry," Rafi said, reading my face.

"It is not a metaphor. It is a swipe," I said. "Hold your loupe and look. The base swirl is the press signature. Fact."

He looked and laughed once. "I see the comma and the slash," he said. "Now I will never unsee it."

I took the ruler card and placed it inside the cup flat against the wall to catch the stain line with a measure again. I snapped two photos. Then I placed the card outside under the handle and captured the hairline and the chip. Then a full profile with the task lamp dimmed one notch to reduce glare. I lay the tent cup beside ours and made a two-cup shot with both bodies in frame and both lines visible. Collages help juries.

Peppermint shoved his nose at the towel and flopped on the stool. He gave a short comment I translated for myself as get on with it.

"Pour line sits higher than tent set," Rafi said for the file, deadpan. "Crazing unique. Hairline on handle matches shop stray. Foot chip matches shop stray. Thumb scuffs near handle match bar crowd habit. Base swirl slash matches previous bar photo. This is our cup."

"Lock the object," I said. "Now we can talk chain."

We keep a binder for housewares used in events. It has nothing to do with town rules. It is about borrowing habits. People like to carry things from counter to tent without asking because they believe in community property until the day it matters. Our binder gives me a sheet for every cup that leaves the building during an event, a joke that went serious after one Thanksgiving when our pie server went to a church and did not come home.

I pulled the sheet for event smallwares. Rafi had logged tent cups out at eleven, return expected at two. He had not logged any shop cups out because none should have walked. He had checked the espresso bar at eleven thirty to clear overflow. At that check he had written one line. Stray cup, sink tray. I touched my finger to the ink without smearing. He fills the book with ballpoint, not gel. It sits firm.

"Check the sink log," I said.

We both looked. Under the same page he had written a usual note. Sink tray: three forks, one butter knife, one stray cup, soaked and air dry by four. I point at my own scribbles and do not apologize. I run a shop by writing it down.

"Tell me about yesterday at four," I said.

He watched the ceiling and played it back. "You asked me to wash the small stack. I rinsed the cup, scrubbed the lip, and set it to drip on the mat. I remember because that hairline grabbed the cloth. I left it on the tray and went to label the cider jugs. I did not move it from the sink to the bar. It did not leave the kitchen in my hands. When I closed, it was back by the espresso bar water station. I assumed you moved it, because I never put that one out."

"I did not," I said. "I do not love chipped ears where customers reach. Someone moved it."

He nodded. "Between four and close," he said. "Or this morning before open."

We leave a small lost and found box in the back hall for bracelets, tote pins, book lights, and strays that migrate off. I checked it last night for any odd parts before bed, an old habit from years of catching forks before the city catches me. I did not check for saucers. That was a miss.

"Flag lost and found," I said.

Rafi was already on the move. He went to the back hall and came back with the little shoebox we use for the week. He set it on the counter and lifted the lid. Inside sat a tangle of small truths. A hair tie. A page flag pad. A children's bracelet with a tiny bell. And a saucer, off-white to the eye, with a small chip under the rim. He held it up. The chip sat in the same place as the cup ear chip if you nested them. That is not science. It is the kind of coincidence that always makes me slow down so I do not rush into a claim. I brought the cup and set it on the saucer. Balance. The foot sat snug. The wobble smoothed because the chip on the saucer made a new seat for the chip on the foot.

Rafi whistled soft. "I bagged this last night," he said. "Donna found it on the romance table under a catalog. I tossed it in the box when I was closing and forgot to mention it in the stack of things you tell me while you clean the grinder."

"You are forgiven," I said. "The room forgives you because you put it in a box and not in the trash."

I lifted the saucer and turned it to the light. The glaze crazing matched the cup class. The pattern on it had a soft wave near one edge where a loop of glaze pooled and pulled fine lines in a tight fan. I checked the back. No maker's mark. One faint ring scuff from where it lived on a metal shelf. I placed it on the towel and set the loupe to the chip. Fresh. The clay under the glaze had the color of a break that did not meet a sink before today. If this chip had lived in river water for months, the edges would have softened. If it had lived in our sink for weeks, it would carry tannin on the raw edge. It looked like the saucer met a table yesterday or the day before.

"Photograph," I said. "Chip. Foot. Overall."

Rafi shot them, then took one of the pair together with the cup nested. He pulled a small label and wrote SAUCER LF-BOX, 10:14, and stuck it to the bag he had used last night. Paper in order saves rooms.

I set the cup and saucer apart again and went to the espresso bar to take the reference shot that would tie this back to our world before the tent. The bar water station sits under a smaller lamp that shows smudges and teaches you humility. I found our usual mark on the counter where the stray cup often sits, a faint ring stain from last week that I had not scrubbed because I had been interrupted mid wipe. The ring had a chip gap in it, a small notch where the ear chip keeps liquid from tracing a perfect circle when a cup is set down too fast. I took that shot, ruler in frame, hearts thumping in my neck because sometimes you get a gift.

"Come here," I called.

Rafi came. He is good at reading my voice when it lowers. He looked at the mark, then looked at the cup. He grinned without showing teeth.

"That is our notch," he said.

"That is our notch," I said.

He wiped the ring with a dry towel and the ghost stayed. He wet the towel and wiped again and the ghost faded but did not die. I took a second shot with the towel mid wipe to show persistence. It would matter less in a lab than in a room where defense loves to suggest I see things I want to see.

I returned to the sink and laid out our lineup on the towel. Cup.

Saucer. Ruler card. Two swabs. Two tent cups. One shot of the bar ring with notch. One of the bar log with my note about the wobble last week. One of the sink log from yesterday. Build the board. Build the day.

Asa came in from the alley with the look he gets when a timeline sits still in his head without protest. He skimmed the counter, the bagged saucer, the cup on the towel, the swabs, the photos, the ruler. He nodded once.

"Tell me in one para," he said.

"Cup is ours," I said. "Glaze pattern unique to our stray. Hairline on handle matches the one that catches our drying cloth. Chip on foot sits at seven. Pour line sits higher than tent cups. Thumb scuffs at handle show bar habit. Base swirl slash matches bar photo. Saucer in lost and found with fresh chip nests the cup and takes its wobble. Bar ring shows a notch that maps to chip. Both have no maker mark. Tent set has a maker ghost and a blue cast. We have the gel note for the pour and a sale tied to Martin for the pen. This object did not start at the tent. It started at our bar."

He ran his finger along the cup rim without touching. He looks like a man making a wish when he does that. It is only a habit with the same shape.

"Bag them separate," he said. "Then bag them together. Photos go both ways. This is good work."

He rested his palm near the towel without leaning on it. "If this cup started at your bar, someone walked it," he said. "Who and when, we can work. The room needs you to hold the thing that touched Harold's mouth. You have it. Keep the chain."

I nodded. Rafi had two bags ready. He slid the cup into a sleeve with anchor points so it would not grind against plastic and make new scratches. He slid the saucer into its own. Then he put both in a larger rigid box with foam corners. He wrote CUP, SAUCER, SHOP STRAY MATCH. He added our initials and the time and the room. He handed me the marker and I did it again. Repetition is not a quirk. It is insurance.

Peppermint stood and stretched his back legs like he had been the one catching evidence. He nosed the foam with respect and decided it did not smell interesting. He released us from his audit and returned to his stool.

I washed my hands and dried them with a fresh towel. The bitter smell had climbed into my sinuses despite my care. I looked at Rafi and saw the same tightness at the corners of his mouth. We work in books and cups because we like rooms that do not hurt anyone. Today we had to hold both.

"Log the saucer bag from last night," I said. "Put the time and the hand that put it in the box."

"Donna," Rafi said, and wrote her name. He added found on romance under a catalog. His handwriting leaned right, steady. He dotted his i after the fact, always two seconds late. He has done that as long as I have known him. It is not a tell. It is a personality tick that makes me fond.

Asa tucked the rigid box under his arm. "I will walk this to the office," he said. "Then I am going to speak to a dry cleaner about a jacket pocket that smells like the inside of your swab tube. We will compare green glows. The picture will get loud."

"Before you go," Rafi said, reaching for the lost and found box. "You should know I bagged this saucer last night because the chip looked new. One more thing. The stick-on dot we use on lost and found items is missing from the sheet. The sheet lived under the counter by the bar. I think whoever moved the cup wiped the bar for a moment and picked up a dot on their sleeve or hand. The dot color is mint. If you see a mint circle on a coat in a photo, you will know it shook hands with our counter."

Asa's mouth twitched, the closest he gets to a smile on a hard day. "You two and your dots," he said. "All right. Mint watch. Noted."

He left. The panel hummed. The cup-shaped space on the towel felt larger than the cup had been. I turned the tent lid hinge notch to ninety and placed the coconut dome like a little moon on the counter for a fresh shot. The city believes what it can see. I hand it bright pictures so it can see.

Rafi set the loupe on its stand and wiped the handle of the faucet until it squeaked. He hates sticky metal. He glanced at Peppermint and then back at me.

"Lock the object," he said.

"Locked," I said.

He stepped to the lost and found shelf to return the box. He stopped, hand hovering over the slot where we put small rings and pins. His face changed by a degree.

"What," I said.

He lifted a tiny circle from the felt. A mint dot, sticky side out, folded in on itself so it looked like a seed. He held it up and turned it in the light.

"Found your mint," he said.

"Bag it," I said.

He did. He labeled it with the location and the minute. He put it with the rest of our day.

I killed the panel to give my eyes a breath. The room softened. The sink looked like a sink again, not a stage. Peppermint jumped down and trotted back toward the front like a man on an errand. Rafi cleaned the towel space and set a fresh one out, habit on habit until we felt human again.

On my way to the door I checked the small lost and found slot again and felt foolish because we had just dug in it, then justified because foolish and careful are cousins. The shelf held nothing new. The box held our saucer bag and a bracelet that would make a child cry tonight and grin tomorrow when it comes home.

I wrote one card for the file and spoke it under my breath as my pen moved. Stray cup matched. Crazing and chip lock to bar. Stain line high. Saucer in lost and found nests chip. Bar ring notch confirms chip map. Chain clean. Then I slid the card into the slot and went to sell a book to a man who needed a story that ends with a kitchen table and a cake that does not fall.

CHAPTER 11

Shelf Sit

The front room had the hush of a church after a bake sale. Powdered sugar still floated in the light near the window, the bell swung on its loop as people edged through with voices tuned low, and the banned table held its line like a teacher who has decided to let discussion breathe. I could feel the town trying to return to normal without lying to itself about what had happened. That is always the balance. Keep the floor steady. Keep the air honest.

I carried the rigid evidence box from the back with the cup and saucer nested in foam and set it on the far end of the counter, well away from the espresso taps. Rafi drew a chalk square on the surface like a polite fence. Donna whispered to a girl about cat stickers. Paula stood near the front display and talked to a father about context without raising her voice. People like paper when the hour shakes.

Peppermint sprang to my shoulder as I crossed the mat and rode me like an admiral until I stepped into the aisle between Cooking and Essays. He hopped down onto the waist-high shelf with the neat row of coil-bound cookbooks and sat. He has a way of finding the square inch where my eye needs to go long before I admit it. I do not give him credit for solving anything. He is a cat. He hunts warm spots and paper with a comfortable give. He nails timing more than facts.

Today he parked himself on a slim book with a green spine and a tomato on the cover. The book lived at eye level beside the banned table because we had pulled together a thread on food writing to soften the hard edges for browsers who needed to rest their eyes before choosing a title with history in it. The book had a sticker from a church sale in the corner. It had no dust jacket. It had been read to death and then kept on a shelf for company. Someone had written a name inside the front leaf and then crossed it out when they gifted it. I like books that carry more than one life on their first page. They forgive a lot.

"Off," I told the cat.

Peppermint groomed one paw and ignored me with grace. His back paw tapped twice. That is his theater. I put two fingers on his shoulder and nudged. He moved exactly six inches and then planted again, as if to say I will concede but I will not retreat.

The book under him sat a fraction forward from its neighbors. Most people slide books flush by habit. When one sticks its nose out you pay attention. The edge of a paper strip peeped from the top as if someone had used a small rectangle as a bookmark and forgot to own the choice. I pinched the strip with nails rather than skin and eased it free one millimeter at a time until the top quarter sat in air. I stopped. Rafi read my body and brought the camera.

"Photo in place," I said.

He shot the spine, the shelf number, the position next to the banned display, and the corner of the strip, nothing else. Then he shot my gloved hand reaching but not touching. Then he shot Peppermint's disinterested face for the card I keep in my mental drawer labeled comic relief that will not taint a chain.

"Bag," I said.

Rafi held a paper sleeve open. I slid the strip out with the tips of my tweezers and let it drop clean. He sealed the flap and labeled the bag with the shelf, the title under it, the time, and the phrase hiding in plain sight. I opened my notebook and wrote the same things in my block letters that never win prizes and always pull their weight.

Then I opened the sleeve and read the strip.

Dry-clean claim ticket. Pinstripe Cleaners, Harbor Avenue. Bold black numbers. Customer: Keene, M. Item: Men's blazer. Tag time: 12:42. Special instructions: inside pocket sticky, rush if possible. The clerk had initialed with a shoulder-wide flourish I see on fast hands that still take pride.

I felt every muscle in my neck try to choose a new shape. The trick is you do not let them. You stay where you are. You keep your voice even. You continue to write clean.

"Read it out," Rafi said, quiet enough that only the ticket and I could hear him.

"Dry-clean claim ticket," I said. "Pinstripe Cleaners. Customer Keene, M. Item: men's blazer. Tag time twelve forty two today. Special instructions mention sticky inner pocket. Rush if possible. Clerk initials are AH."

Rafi said nothing for three seconds, which is his way of letting me decide if we run or walk. The tent camera time on the thud had sat at twelve twenty six by our grid. The alley camp said close enough. The bake tent hummed through twelve thirty with chatter that tasted like grief and frosting. The dry cleaner logged a blazer sixteen minutes later with a note you do not see on a shirt that just got butter on it.

"Eyes only for now," I said. "No show and tell."

"Agreed," he said.

I photographed the ticket in its sleeve with my ruler card and a corner of the cookbook cover in frame. Then I took a shot of the shelf position beside the banned table and the line of sight from the cash wrap so a stranger could understand how easy it would be to tuck something while pretending to browse. I wrote down the title under the strip. Casseroles for Busy Nights. I wrote the author. I wrote the price. I wrote the note that the inside front leaf carries two names, one crossed out. No detail is too small when someone makes a strange choice standing right next to a display that already agitates half a town.

"Who put hands on this shelf in the last hour," I asked.

"Three mothers, one father, Nina for a second and then she refused to look at recipes because she said sugar was a gateway," Donna said from the register, because she had a mind like a tape. "Paula shelved two returns. A pair of teens took a selfie with a pie book and then put it back wrong, and I fixed it. Martin stopped in for ten seconds and looked at the banned table and then at the open spot in the ring where Harold fell. He did not touch a book."

I let my eyes slide to the front door. The bell had rung for him a half hour ago. He had stood exactly where the dry-clean ticket had lived. He had not reached for the book because he had no intention of pretending to read. He had tilted his head half an inch and smiled at a line in air only he could see. Then he had left as if pulled by magnet.

"Who else with him," I said.

"No one," Donna said. "He walked in alone. He looked alone. He left alone."

Paula stepped beside me and read the line on the slip through the sleeve with the cold careful expression she uses to protect the part of her that speaks in rooms for a living. "Sticky inner pocket," she said, as if tasting the words. "You bring that sentence into a jury and even the soft heart in the back row will lean forward."

"I am not carrying this to any jury," I said. "I am carrying it to Asa. First I am going to shore up the chain and put a phone call on tape."

Rafi nodded and made a neat pile on the counter. Ticket. Photo of the shelf. Photo of the sleeve with the ruler. Card with my hand. He placed Peppermint's tired face aside for later. We do not need a cat for chain. We need clean corners.

"Bag anything else from the spot," I said.

He slid a clean piece of paper under the sliver of shelf where the ticket had rested and lifted gently so he could catch any dust or fiber. He folded the paper and put it in a small envelope labeled sweep. He initialed and dated. He walked the sweep to the back and popped it into the rigid box with the cup and saucer so the story could travel together even if we needed to split for errands.

A woman stopped at the banned table with a furrowed look and read the placard about context while her toddler hummed at a picture on a cover. Paula stepped forward and offered a hand without tension. The woman started to speak, faltered, then smiled and said thank you and moved on. I watched her hands. Empty. No tucking. No shifts. No heat.

Rafi returned and stood at my side with the expression that means I am here for the next move. He flicked his eyes at the ticket sleeve and then at my phone. He wanted me to make the call. He wanted my voice on the record with a time and a sentence that would bring a coat to a counter.

"Do it now," he said.

I dialed Pinstripe Cleaners from the number on the ticket. The ring had the thin tone that tells you the line is old and the bell inside is older.

"Pinstripe," a woman said, bright. "Angie speaking."

"Hi, Angie," I said. "This is Liora from Peppermint Cat. I have a question and a favor. Do you have a moment."

"For you, sure," she said. "Want me to pull the theatre drape again. Those loops like to jump."

"Different errand," I said. "I need a rush pickup for a test spot. I can bring it to you if you cannot come here. I am on clock."

"We can send Jules in ten, unless he is stuck behind a bus on Harbor," she said. "What is the garment and what is the enemy. Coffee. Wine. The pink napkins. I told the church to stop buying the pink napkins."

"I have a silk scarf with a bitter spill," I said, telling the truth in shape if not the whole line. "Small. I want to see if your solvent lifts it clean without a ring. I need you to tag it and turn it fast so I can show a result to a person who screams when you use the wrong cleaner."

"Story of my day," she said. "Bring it or wait for Jules. He is out now. He can swing by if you throw me a curbside."

"I will bring it," I said. "I will be there in eight. While I have you, did you tag a men's blazer at twelve forty two with a note about a sticky inner pocket. I am not asking for details. I am asking to plan around your rack if you have a chemical set up."

She paused, the kind of pause that holds three thoughts and a glance at a screen. "We did," she said. "Light gray blazer. Pocket liner with a tacky lip. I told the customer I would have to ask the owner about the best attack because I do not want to melt a lining to save a dollar. I do not plan to touch it until the owner looks."

"Owner in," I said.

"He is on a pickup run," she said. "Back by one. We tagged the blazer with rush because the customer did that face where he says the word event. The tag says Keene."

"Thank you," I said. "I will bring the scarf and not breathe on your racks."

"You never breathe on my racks," she said. "You bring cookies at Christmas and your notes do not smear. I like you. See you in eight."

I ended the call and wrote the line on my card. Pinstripe confirms blazer tag at 12:42. Sticky inner pocket noted. Owner not yet in. Rush requested by customer. I slid the card under the ticket sleeve on the counter and took a shot of both to close the loop on that first pass. Then I put my phone face down and looked at the book that had hidden the slip.

"Who shelved this," I asked Donna.

"Yesterday," she said. "It came in with a box from Mrs. Leary. She gets church sale boxes when they do the spring cull. I wiped the cover and set it here because I wanted soup near the archive table for mood. No one bought it. I saw no one nest a slip between pages until now."

"Mrs. Leary brings lemon squares every third week," Rafi added, because he tracks sugar the way I track paper.

I opened the book to the place where the ticket had lived. The page held a recipe for a casserole that claimed to feed eight and would feed six if anyone in the room had any kind of appetite. A grease oval sat on the bottom margin, old and honest. No fresh blot. No wet. The ticket had slipped between clean pages. The strip had no smear from butter. The hands that hid it did not have sauce on them. Small, but I wrote it down. People notice later when you can say a thing like that without effort.

Peppermint stood up and circled exactly once on the shelf, then stepped onto the top of the banned table placard and sat. The top edge of the sign dipped under his weight and then held. He flicked his tail twice and looked past me toward the door as if expecting a parade.

"Off," I said again. He yawned and got off in slow motion and found a place on the mat where he could own the doorway without risking toes. He is vain. He is my cat.

Paula leaned closer to the shelf and read the recipe line. "Mrs. Leary will argue about the salt," she said. "She always does. She does not write slips into books. She keeps a clutch of lined paper in her tote. I have borrowed it too many times to forget the feel. Whoever tucked this had a claim to hide. He could have shoved it into his own pocket. He could not. Sticky liner. He took a book and made it a pocket that would not contaminate his shirt."

"He did it standing where we can see him," I said. "And where a camera can see him. We have that little dome at the corner for shrink. It took a sweep about the time he walked in. I will pull it after we get the scarf in motion."

"You need backup," Paula said.

"I need you to keep the room calm while we run two blocks,"

I said. "Rafi will stay. I will go. Donna will watch my counter. Peppermint will supervise without shame."

Peppermint chirped at his name and tried to step onto the evidence box. Rafi moved the box a foot and the cat accepted the compromise with bad grace. Donna handed me a scarf from the prop basket in the office because presentation matters even when the scarf is bait. She chose the red one that bleeds if you look at it wrong. Pinstripe knows better than to use a cleaner that eats dye. Angie can make a ring disappear that would give a lesser cleaner nightmares. I have seen her fix a disaster more than once. I trust her. I do not need to tell her why this scarf is more than a scarf. I will anyway, in simple, because I want the owner to set his eyes on a blazer with care.

"Paula," I said, "if someone asks, say out loud that the table stays and that donations go in the jar in bills and that ledger lines get written by the person logged as clerk. Say it five times if you need to. The hour loves to spin. Tethers help."

She nodded, then took the banned table placard from the stand and wiped the top edge where Peppermint hairs had landed. She set it back without a hair on it. She runs a room the way she runs a ledger. Clean edges. Firm lines. No drama unless the story asks for it.

I put the scarf in a zip bag with a note on a card. Test spot, silk. Request: lift bitter residue without ring. Document process. Please call before heat. I signed my name and wrote the shop number and my personal number and Asa's card number in the corner. I can get a cleaner to call me back. Asa has a better pull if someone wants to feel official. I added "this is a favor for a fast learning situation" and left it at that. You do not put the word case on paper until you have to.

"Keys," Rafi said.

I patted my pocket, showed him the ring, and took a breath that tasted like cinnamon and strong coffee. The room can survive without me for ten minutes. It has done it before. It will do it again.

"Donna," I said, "if Nina comes in and asks to move the placards to the back, you tell her no and offer a cookie. If she throws a line about harm, you tell her to ask Paula to define terms. If she raises her voice, you tap the bell three times and I will appear like a card trick."

"She can have a macaroon if she pays for it," Donna said.

"She can," I said.

I tucked the ticket sleeve into a hard case with the scarf so it would travel even if a careless driver took a corner too fast. I wrote a quick chain card for the countertop. Ticket discovered in cookbook at 13:06. Bagged and photographed. Call to Pinstripe at 13:09. Rush test requested. Blazer tag confirmed. Owner out. We go at 13:12. I left it on the counter by the chalk square and tapped it twice because I am allowed one private superstition.

At the door I looked back. The banned table stood without anyone kneeling to rip it apart. Paula fielded a question from a mother with patience that did not taste like sugar. Rafi checked the espresso wand and wiped the steam arm with a clean cloth. Peppermint blinked at me with a face that said go bring back something interesting. Shelves held. People held. It would do.

I pushed the door with my hip and stepped into sun that had decided to show up for the first time in an hour. Harbor Avenue wore the light like a shirt it had not expected to fit. Across the street the flags over the diner made a small clack and then hung again. Pinstripe Cleaners sits two blocks over, impossible to miss because the awning is green and the front window holds a mannequin in a tuxedo that has been there since I moved here. The tuxedo never changes. The hand-lettered sign under it shifts with the week. Today it said Fast Hands, Gentle Soap.

I walked fast without looking like I was running from a crime. People read speed. They read faces. You learn to carry a neutral face when the world starts taking sides. I kept my eyes up and my shoulders level and thought about a silk scarf heavy with dye and the hands that know how to coax a stain out without shredding truth.

At the corner I stopped myself from planning the next three moves in a row. That is how you trip. The next move is the call I already made. The next act is to walk in and set the scarf down and watch Angie watch it. The act after that is to ask about buffers and see what her eyes do when I describe the smell on my swab in technical words instead of kitchen words. I can talk both. People forget that about shopkeepers. We check inventory and read science and talk money with the same mouth. We keep a town going because we never get to pick one lane.

I reached for the door, then stopped to speak to a camera mounted above the jamb. I like to declare time twice when rooms shift into places where people wear uniforms. "Leaving Peppermint Cat at one twelve," I said, low. "Ticket bagged. Calling cleaner. Scarf in hand. On record." I do not know if anyone watches my cameras in real time. I watch myself on playback to keep my steps honest.

The bell over the door gave a clean note when I grabbed the handle. I pulled the door open and stepped through and the air smelled like starch and lemon. Angie looked up from the press, lifted a hand, and smiled in a way that made the room feel like a place where mistakes still have a path home. I lifted the bag with the scarf.

"Help me with a rush test," I said.

"You got it," she said.

The rest would live in the next room. For now I had my end hook and my next call on tape. I turned my head toward the street and said one more sentence for the day.

"Pinstripe," I said into my phone log, loud enough that Rafi would hear if he played it back in an empty shop. "I am here. I need your best work."

CHAPTER 12

Claim Ticket

P instripe Cleaners smells like starch, lemon, and the kind of heat that smooths a day whether it wants to smooth or not. I pushed through the door with the red silk scarf in a clear bag and the dry-clean claim ticket in a labeled sleeve. The bell on the frame gave a brisk note I heard over presses that sighed and snapped like calm surf.

Angie stood at the counter in her crisp apron with a pencil behind one ear. She had a stack of claim envelopes on her left, a stapler on her right, and the open book they use to copy tag numbers by hand when the computer throws a fit. Her hair was up in a knot that meant work, not a show. She smiled when she saw me and slid the book away from the edge so I would not knock it with my elbow.

"You made it in seven," she said. "I owe Jules coffee. He guessed ten."

"He will survive without winning," I said, and set the bag on the counter. "Here is the scarf. Silk. Bright dye. I need your best work on a small test spot. Light touch. No ring."

"We like silk that screams," she said. "It keeps us awake."

She set the scarf on a white board and leaned close without touching. "I see one dull crescent near the edge of the border," she said. "That looks like the spot you want lifted. I will patch test and keep the edge wet so a ring does not draw a map. If a ring thinks about forming, I stop. I like to keep silk safe from heroics."

"Good," I said. "I also need to look at a blazer tagged twelve forty two. Light gray. Keene. The claim ticket was tucked in a cookbook beside my banned table. I have the sleeve here. I can wait if you need the owner in the room."

She watched my face the way a person watches for a lie. I let her read nothing but the hour. The hour always writes across my jaw when a room asks for a steady hand.

"We logged that jacket after lunch rush," she said. "Tag says twelve forty two. The note says sticky inner pocket. I did not dig in. A pocket liner that grabs your glove means pause. Mr. DeLuca likes to look at anything odd before I start."

"Can I see it," I asked. "I will not touch without gloves. I will not let air make trouble. I am here as a person with a chain, not a thief with a hunch."

She weighed that and then nodded. "You are on my list of people who bring cookies in December and who write names on bags that do not smear," she said. "I will pull it. If my boss walks in, he will speak to you before he speaks to me and I will hold that against him for five minutes."

She stepped to the rolling rack with fresh tags and slid hangers with the practiced flick of someone who can read numbers without saying them out loud. She stopped at a light gray blazer with a tag that matched the claim ticket in my sleeve. She wheeled it to the counter and let it rest in the valley of the wood so the weight would not pull the shoulders. Her hands are kind to garments. You can see that kindness in how cloth relaxes for her.

"Here it is," she said. "We gave it the first look and stopped. The pocket tack felt odd through the lining. I did not reach inside. I took one whiff and parked it. The note is mine because I do not trust my memory on days like this."

She turned the tag so I could see the number, the time, the initials AH. I slid the sleeve with the ticket beside it and took a clean photo of both, ruler card in frame, with her permission and with the counter edge visible for context. I wrote the time on my card and underlined it. Twelve forty two. We had the collapse at twelve twenty six by the tent camera and the front room clock. Sixteen minutes from a fall to a tag.

"Gloves," I said.

She handed me a box of nitrile and I pulled two. I do not touch anyone's clothes with bare skin, and I never touch a pocket lip bare when a note on a tag says sticky. I held the hanger and let the blazer rest while I leaned in. Up close, the wool carried a faint clean scent from a wear that does not sit in smoke. The inside of the pocket had a different story. A faint bitter smell lived there, like the ghost of a bad almond under starch. My throat tightened on reflex. I do not name a thing like that in a shop. I let the room be light and heat and lemon.

"Describe it," Angie said.

"Faint," I said. "Bitter. Not kitchen. Not citrus. Not wine. Not coffee. Not grease. Your note hit the word sticky for a reason."

"Yes," she said. "When I pressed the lining with the tip of my nail it grabbed as if a child had dragged his hand through something sweet and then patted his pocket for a marble. It pulled and then released with a tack. I did not want that in our drum."

"Good call," I said.

I took a fresh cotton swab from my kit, opened the paper sleeve without breathing on the stick, and rolled the cotton once along the inner lip of the pocket seam where fabric meets fabric. The cotton took nothing a person would see with an eye. It does not need to. I placed the swab tip against a quick test strip from my case, the same kind we used on the cup rim in the back sink, and watched the patch. The square shifted to green. Not a paint job, not a wash. A clean change you can photograph without explanations and a good light.

I set the strip on the counter next to today's newspaper and took the shot with a straight angle and no hero shadows. I wrote the time on the card beside it and then slid the swab into a labeled tube for Asa. I put the used strip into a zipper bag with the label in frame and a note on the outside with my initials and Angie's initials. Angie watched my hands without flinching. She has iron when she needs it. She has taste for procedure when a room demands it.

"We logged the blazer after the collapse," she said, as if helping me keep a chain straight even when it was already straight. "The tag time is computer. I wrote the note with my pen. He walked in with the jacket over his arm and asked for rush. He kept talking about an event and a photo. He did not say funeral. He did not say name. He asked if we could turn it before dinner."

"Deposit," I asked.

"Ten," she said, and slid the receipt book from under the counter. She opened to the page where a thin carbon copy sat under a top sheet and tapped the line with a nail. Keene, M. Ten on account. Rush on blazer, sticky pocket liner, owner to inspect before treatment. She folded the top sheet over and tore along the perforation and let me look without touching. The time matched the tag. The number matched the claim. She loved that kind of match and so do I. She offered to copy. I said Asa would bring a form and a calm voice and she smiled because she knows him too.

"Owner name," I said. "Mr. DeLuca today or his father."

"Son," she said. "He grew up behind this counter. He does not lose his head for stain talk. He has rules for pockets. He will take that jacket into the back and hold the lining to the light and make a face only cleaning people understand."

"Where is he," I asked.

"Pickup run," she said. "Council building and two suits from Harbor Bank. He will be back before one. He will grumble about traffic and then eat a sandwich in three bites and pretend he chews five. He will look at this liner before anything else."

"Good," I said.

I called Asa before I touched anything else. He answered on the second ring and saved his words.

"Pinstripe," I said. "Blazer tag twelve forty two, Keene. Pocket liner tacky. Faint bitter smell. Test strip shifted green on a swab from the inner lip. I have photos with today's paper and the tag. Angie logged a deposit at the same time. Owner on way in. We need you here for the move. I will not let the jacket leave this counter without you and a receipt."

"Hold the space," he said. "I am two blocks out."

He arrived in under three minutes, which means he was closer than two blocks. He walked in without tread and did not look at the rack first. He looked at the counter, the blazer, the tag, my sleeve, the test strip bag, the tube, and Angie's face. He gave her the nod he uses for civilians who save him hours.

"Thank you," he said.

"I did not dig in," she said. "I did not want it in my drum or near my solvents until you two spoke in full sentences."

He gave a small bow with his eyes. "Can you hold a line out front if I bring the owner into the back for a look," he said. "I will log a transfer for the jacket so we do not break your paper."

She lifted the counter flap and waved him through like a person opening a gate at a track. "My machine is hot," she said. "We can stamp anything you bring."

Mr. DeLuca stepped in on the sentence, keys in hand, collar half unbuttoned from his run. He saw the angle of the room in one glance and slipped behind the counter where the blazer rested. He held the hanger like it was a bird he wanted to calm.

"What have we got," he said.

"Customer brought this at twelve forty two," Angie said. "Sticky pocket liner. I paused. Liora brought a test. The patch turned green. Deputy Hale wants to take the jacket with a receipt. He will hold paper."

Mr. DeLuca breathed in at the pocket lip, wrinkled his nose in a way his father taught him, and nodded once.

"I was going to park it on the quarantine rack anyway," he said. "I do not love a pocket that grabs a glove. I do not love a smell that sets on my tongue. You can take it if you promise me a process that respects cloth. I have friends who work in suits that cost more than my rent and they still spill dressing. I know my trade. I also know when to stop pretending I am a hero."

"You will get a receipt," Asa said. "We will keep it hung and safe. You will get photos when we return it. Your carbon stays complete."

Angie brought out a blank receipt form for transfers, the one they use when a garment goes to a specialist. She slapped it down in front of Mr. DeLuca and reached for her pen. He wrote the tag number, the time, the words hold for deputy in neat letters, and signed. Asa wrote his name and badge number. I wrote mine as witness and added Peppermint Cat as a third line because my shop floats in a lot of rooms like a cork. We are good at holding shape.

Mr. DeLuca unhooked the blazer from the intake rack and put it on a clean hanger from the back, then slipped a paper shoulder guard over it so sunlight would not fade it while we stood in the doorway. He slid a garment bag over the whole frame and handed Asa the hook.

"Treat the cloth like a person," he said. "Do not fold the lapel wrong. Do not crush the shoulders. Do not let someone throw it in a tub. If you need to swab again, pull the lining away from the wool so the sample does not wick."

"I will keep it dressed," Asa said.

I took two photos of the bagged jacket on the counter with the transfer receipt in the corner and Angie's initial by the time. Then I stepped back so I did not crowd anyone. Angie went to set the scarf on a board at a tank where she keeps test bottles.

She ran a small bead of her mildest solvent along a border with a feather brush and watched the line. It lifted a shade and she smiled at the way dye held its stance.

"Your scarf will live," she said. "It will be brighter on that edge by two degrees. I will feather the edges so no one sees where I was."

"You are a wonder," I said.

"I am a person who learned the hard way not to chase a stain across a field," she said. "We keep a town presentable by moving slow."

The bell over the door gave a new note that did not match the last eight customers. A head in the doorway can carry a chord. This one had an overtone that sounded like theater. Martin Keene stepped through with a look that put surprise on top of worry like a glaze you hope will hide a flaw. He took in the room, saw me, saw Asa, saw the bagged blazer on the counter, and shaped his mouth into a neat O.

"Oh," he said. "You are here."

Angie looked at me and then at the rack of claim tags and did not lift a finger to cover anything. Mr. DeLuca set his shoulders and did not step away from the counter. Asa did not adjust his stance. He does not widen or puff. He stands like a tree that knows wind will come.

"I came to check on a jacket," Martin said. "I stained it. I need it for tonight."

"Tag number," Angie said, as if she did not have the ticket number wired into her brain. Her face stayed calm. I loved her for it.

Martin reached into his pocket and then remembered his claim slip was not in his pocket, because the pocket had been too sticky for his nerves, and then remembered where he had tucked it. He flicked his eyes at the shelf where the cookbook had lived beside my banned table and then snapped back to the counter as if he had never looked away.

"I lost the slip," he said, with a small shrug you learn in meetings where you want a room to forgive a blank line. "I figured you could find me. Keene. Martin."

Angie lifted the carbon copy and placed it on the counter with one finger. "We found you at twelve forty two," she said. "We logged your jacket. We noted the pocket. We marked rush. Owner to inspect before treatment. You are on the board whether you like it or not."

He started to speak and then stopped when Asa turned the garment bag so the transfer receipt faced the room. The line hold for deputy sits plain even when you want it to hide. Martin blinked twice and put a hand on the counter in the universal gesture that tries to steady a situation without helping it one bit.

"I do not understand," he said. "Why is there a deputy here. Why is my jacket in a bag. I came to pick it up. We have a dinner. We have people coming."

"You asked for rush," Angie said. "We set rush. The pocket liner carries a tack. We paused. You did not pick up a clean thing. You brought a problem. We call problems by name in this room."

Asa slid his card across the counter without force. "We need to speak about your jacket and a cup," he said. "Not here at a counter. In a room where paper lives."

Martin looked at me then, as if I had built this entire scene to hurt his schedule. He tried a smile that had charmed donors more times than I care to count. It failed on the glass of this counter and fell to the floor with a soft clink only I heard.

"I am surprised to see you here," he said. "I was coming anyway."

"I do not chase stains in silence," I said. "You taught me that with your advisory fund speeches."

Angie put the scarf in a mesh cradle and lowered it into a bath that knew how to treat silk. She watched for a ring and saw none, because she knows how to work and because the room had decided to show us one small kindness. Mr. DeLuca picked up a brown paper sack with two sandwiches and walked it to the back so he would not have to watch a man pretend he had never heard the word sticky. Asa wrote a receipt for the jacket transfer and had Angie stamp it with the green seal that lives in a drawer for rare days. The seal leaves a concentric ring on paper like the grip mark a careful glass leaves on a linen cloth.

Martin put his hands flat on the wood. He wanted to speak and he did not know which line would save him. You learn to see that moment in people who think language can bend time. He looked at the bag with a knot between his eyes and then said a thing he thought belonged on the set of a tidy movie.

"I spilled tea," he said. "I tried to wipe it. I came here because I trust your work. That is the whole story."

"It is not," I said. "But it is a start."

CHAPTER 13

Residue Test

The office sits above the alley like a watch box. Narrow window, two file cabinets, one poster from a poetry night, and a desk that belongs to paper first, coffee second. I unlocked the door with my left hand and kept my right around the rigid evidence box like it might jump. Asa followed with the garment bag over his arm. He does not look like a man carrying a hook. He looks like a man carrying a promise.

Rafi had already cleared the desk. Fresh white butcher paper covered the surface in two layers, taped at the corners, seams labeled with the minute. The task lamp stood to my left, the color panel set to noon so glare would not pick fights with my camera. He had placed the evidence sleeves from the sink on the blotter in a neat row. Swab tube from the cup rim. Strip bag from the blazer pocket. Photo of the first shift to green next to today's paper. Empty tubes, clean swabs, ruler card, gloves, two markers, and a clean waste bag folded small like a napkin. He had also peeled a tiny mint dot and stuck it to the top left corner of the butcher paper as a private joke. It steadied me.

Peppermint jumped onto the chair and decided the arms were his throne. He made a softer sound than usual, a noise that fits rooms where glass and words share space. He knows when to be quiet. He does not know why, only that the air asks for it.

"Asa," I said, "hang the blazer on the office rack and let the bag fall to the floor, not the desk."

He did it without asking why. He tries not to put cloth near my camera when the lens is loaded. He sealed the office door and drew the blind on the narrow window. He stood to the side of the desk like a wall that breathes.

"Rafi," I said, "open a new page in the chain. Cup, saucer, blazer, cleaner receipt, strip image from Pinstripe, today's paper. Add my scarf request and Angie's patch result."

Rafi wrote in a steady block hand. He titles his pages with the date and a short word because he is a cook by training and it pleases him to keep labels plain. Today's page read TEA. Under it he listed time marks. 12:26 collapse at tent by front camera. 12:42 blazer checked in at Pinstripe by Angie. 1:09 call to Pinstripe, rush test requested. 1:12 arrival at Pinstripe. 1:18 first office setup. 1:22 transfer receipt stamped. 1:33 return to office. He turned the notebook so I could read and initial. I did.

I put on fresh gloves. The latex snapped once, a sound that tells you your skin is still yours. I opened the rigid box from the sink, lifted the smaller inner sleeves, and laid them along the top of the butcher paper so the labels would sit clear in the camera frame. I opened the garment bag only far enough to free the hanger hook, then lifted the bag's hem so air would not wash over the pocket mouth. Rafi stepped in and clipped a binder clip on the hem to keep it from slumping.

"Call out your steps," Asa said, not because he thought I would forget, but because he knows my voice brings rooms into line.

"Photograph the scene," I said, and Rafi took the shot. "Photograph the newspaper," and he set The Beacon on the left with the masthead visible. "Photograph the ruler card," and he set it next to the paper. "Photograph the test strip from Pinstripe," and he placed the sealed strip bag by the paper and card. I framed it all with the task lamp and took two shots of my own in case someone argued later that I prefer other people's eyes. I do not. I prefer doubles.

I took a clean swab and set it on a tray. I took a new test strip from the foil sleeve and set it at the edge of the paper so I would not smear it with an elbow. I put the cup sleeve on the right and opened it like a book. The rim still carried a faint ring of tan under the bright. Our sink had rinsed the stain, not the history. I rolled a second clean swab over the far side of the rim where lip and glaze meet. I did not use the same spot as the first test. I do not stack samples like cards in a trick deck.

The cotton collected air and a taste of tannin, invisible to eyes, enough for chemistry. I pressed the swab to the test strip and counted to five. The square that starts ghost white darkened, then went soft green that felt like a memory. The exact shade from the pocket test. Not mint, not pine, something in the family of a traffic light at dawn. I felt the small pull over my heart that happens when one answer maps to another without protest.

Rafi leaned in with the camera. He framed the strip with the newspaper masthead and the ruler card and the rim of the cup blurred in the back. He shot, then shot again with the lamp dimmed one notch to take glare off the square, then shot a third with the task lamp moved a finger closer to the strip. He stepped back and let me place the strip into a zipper bag that already wore a label with the time. I initialed. He initialed. We dated the bag and placed it next to the first strip bag from Pinstripe.

"Describe the color," Asa said.

"Green shift, specific grade," I said. "Matches the first shift from the blazer pocket lip. Shot beside the paper for the record. See frame C thirteen through C fifteen."

He nodded and wrote that in his own book. He writes slower than Rafi. He does not care. He cares that his hand does not lie.

I did a control that will save a fight later. I took a swab and rolled it over a clean porcelain ramekin from the office shelf that has never held tea. I pressed it to a fresh strip. The square sat white like snow. I photographed it with the ruler card and the paper. I marked it CLEAN CONTROL in block letters and bagged it. Control saved argument. I like to select fights. I do not like to give them away.

I took another clean strip and used the swab from the blazer pocket tube that we had capped at Pinstripe. I pressed the cotton to the square and watched the shift again. Same tone, same speed. I filmed it with my phone for good measure, because juries trust motion, even if I wish they did not. Rafi took stills while the square bloomed. He set the second strip by the first and wrote BLAZER SWAB SECOND on the bag before the ink could run into the plastic stress.

"Any reason to retest the saucer," Asa asked.

"None," I said. "We do not drink from saucers. The mouth touched the cup. The pocket carried the tool that touched the cup. The strip sings the same note for both. Test the saucer when you need to prove it sat in our lost and found. Not today."

He nodded again, a rhythm that made the room quieter. He glanced at the blazer and then looked away as a courtesy to the cloth. He treats jackets like they have a spine. I respect that.

I set the cup back into its sleeve. I sealed the sleeve and wrote CUP RIM RETEST, GREEN MATCH, beside the time mark. I took the newspaper and folded it so the masthead and the date sat big in the frame, then laid it beside the two strip bags. I photographed both strip bags beside the masthead so a stranger could see without reading a thread. I added the ruler card to that frame again and took one more shot. I put the paper in a new sleeve for this file. I do not like to leave a record loose where a wind gust or a careless hand can go to work.

Peppermint stretched and settled into the chair like a critic who had decided the show would do. He blinked at Asa's shoes. Asa ignored him with respect. I pulled the window blind up a notch to get a reading of the outside color. Clouds had shifted and the street sat in that late noon light that flattens everything. It would cancel glare on the glass if I needed a shot from a different angle. I did not. I let the blind fall.

"Chain," I said.

Rafi read back the line as if presenting a dish. "Cup rim swabbed with clean swab. Strip bloom to green. Photo next to The Beacon masthead and ruler. Second test on blazer pocket swab, same bloom, same photo pairing. Control on clean ramekin, no bloom. All three bagged, labeled, initialed. Cup re-sleeved, saucer untouched. Newspaper sleeved. Camera numbers logged."

"Good," I said.

I felt the tightness in the room change. It is a small thing. The first time you feel it you think it is your stomach. The fourth time you know it is the room letting go because numbers line up. The fact is a fact. There is no need for speeches.

The phone on the corner of the desk buzzed with a text. Angie sent a photo of the scarf on the board. The crescent stain had faded to a whisper. The dye held. She had feathered the edges clean. The caption read: Silk safe. No ring. Back to you in twenty. Under it she had added a small green dot and a smile. I showed it to Rafi and to Asa. He gave a one word answer that worked instead of any sermon.

"Good," he said.

We had to move the objects to his custody next. I do not like to see my sleeves leave the office. I like the feeling of them in the safe. I also like truth more than comfort.

"Asa," I said, "you sign for the cup, the saucer, the two strip bags, the swab tube, the blazer, the transfer receipt, the Pinstripe photo, the newspaper sleeve, and the mint dot if you want it."

"I want it," he said.

Rafi slid a three part receipt pad from the drawer. He wrote each item on a separate line with tag numbers where we had them and a short noun where we did not. I initialed as sender. He signed as witness. Asa printed his name in block letters and added his badge number. He put the first copy into his folder, the second into our drawer, and the third under the desk blotter for the person who will sit here tomorrow when the day tries to run ahead. We run after enough things already. We do not let paper join them.

I lifted the cup sleeve and set it into the rigid box. I set the saucer bag beside it with foam corners so it would not slide and chip. I added the two strip bags, then the swab tube in a small foam cradle. Rafi closed the box and taped the seam twice. He wrote a seal time and signed across the tape. Asa put the box into a canvas evidence tote with a hard bottom. He placed the garment bag with the blazer on his arm like a coat in winter. He placed the newspaper sleeve and the Pinstripe transfer receipt into a flat folder and slid the folder into the tote pocket.

"Anything else," he said.

"Two small things," I said. "Write on your card that Angie froze work on the blazer until you called. Write that Mr. DeLuca signed a transfer and can testify to the smell and the tack. Write that the scarf lifted without a ring so no one thinks we staged a test to frame a cloth. It spares us a speech later."

"I already have them," he said.

He turned to the door. Before he reached for the knob, my office phone rang with the clatter that belongs to landlines that refuse to leave their era. I picked up with the line we use when we want to be polite but leave a space for clarity.

"Peppermint Cat office," I said. "This is Liora."

The voice on the other end had that smooth that people practice in boardrooms so they can sound like help while they do containment. It said its name. It said its firm. It said Martin's name. It said the phrase representation and asked where to send a letter. It asked that all communication go through their office. It asked with care. It asked like a blanket.

"I am in a room with a deputy," I said. "He has the items he needs. He can give you an email. We will honor your request. We will also follow the chain we have already set. You understand."

The voice said the words you expect. Full cooperation. Deep sorrow. Respect for process. A hope for privacy. I wrote the name, the number, and the time. I asked if they would like to confirm that they had spoken to their client before noon about any matter related to today's event. The silence had a weight. Then the voice said they would get back to me with anything they found. That meant no.

"Thank you," I said, and hung up without a speech.

"Martin hired counsel," I said to Asa. "They want email. They want chain. I gave them your card in shape. They did not know about noon. That tells me their seat at the table is new."

He nodded. He did not change his face. He has had more lawyers in his day than I have had poets. He lifted the tote and the blazer and went to the door. He paused long enough to give me a line that I keep in my pocket for ugly afternoons.

"You did the work," he said. "We will carry it."

Rafi walked him down. I sat for one minute with my hands flat on the butcher paper to feel the table hold. Peppermint moved from the chair arm to the blotter and put his paw on the edge of the evidence receipt like a king on a treaty. He purred once and then stopped, as if he had been caught being kind.

I stood and rolled the butcher paper neatly from the far edge toward me so that the surface collected any dust or stray fiber rather than flipping it into the air. I taped the roll and wrote a note on the outside. Office desk cover, test day, C thirteen chain, no visible debris. I slid it into a long bag and wrote the time.

Rafi returned and leaned in the doorway. "He did not look back," he said of Asa. "He rarely does when he leaves with something that matters."

"Martin called a lawyer," I said.

"Good," Rafi said. "He can stop pretending he is still browsing."

We stood a minute more, quiet on purpose. Then I pulled a fresh stack of donation envelopes from the drawer for the counter because people will keep trying to give and you have to give them a clean line to do it. I slid my notebook toward me and wrote the last lines of the hour without dressing them. Cup rim matches blazer pocket by strip bloom. Photo with masthead taken. Control held. Chain closed to Hale. Counsel engaged by Keene. I underlined chain once and drew a small box next to it. I drew a checkmark in the box because I allow myself one moment of kindergarten on days when kindergarten would have saved people if they had listened.

Peppermint jumped down and trotted to the door like a messenger out of an old play. He stopped at the top of the stairs and looked back to see if I was coming. I was. I shut the lamp, locked the drawers, slid my key back into my pocket, and followed him out. I grabbed a tissue on the way and dabbed one spot under my thumb where a green square had tried to hold on. It did not. Some colors do not belong on skin.

Downstairs the bell gave me that one note that still reminds me why I open the door every morning. Donna handed a child a sticker of a cat in space and the child laughed at the helmet. Paula folded a flyer about next month's read and placed it in a stack without nudging corners. The banned table stood exactly where I left it. The town will argue later. Today it would be fine. Rafi wiped the espresso counter and set two cups on a tray for a pair who needed a place to sit. He looked up at me and then at the clock and then at the notebook in my hand. He does not have to ask. He knows.

"Strip sang," I said. "Twice. Same tune."

He smiled without teeth. "Good," he said. "Now we feed whoever forgot lunch."

We did. We fed them. We poured. We handed out napkins. We kept the line short. We gave a woman a chair near the window and we gave her husband a book about a man who builds a boat in a garage for twenty years and never lets anyone tell him he cannot. I put the cup and the saucer in my head in a box that will stay closed until a judge opens it. I put the blazer on a hook in my mind that will not bend. I put the strip color in the slot where I keep hues I never want on a table full of cookies. Then I went back to my counter and sold a paperback to a teenager who had decided that a banned book with a kind spine will do more for him than a rant. He was right.

Near two fifteen my phone trilled again. Angie sent a second photo. The scarf lay on white with a towel under it and no ring in sight. Her caption read: Edgeback perfect. Come by when you can. I typed a thanks and three hearts because sometimes you put sugar on a thing that deserves it.

On the way to the front door to flip the chalkboard from Bake Tent in back to Event paused I took one last look at the office stairs and told myself the next scene would belong to another room. Asa would carry the words forward. I had done my part. The test had tied hand to cup without shouting. That is what this series always asks of me. Prove, not perform. Keep the cat on camera for timing and not for genius. Keep my chain straight.

At the door I touched the chalk frame and wrote one small line underneath the pause. Office closed for one hour earlier to help a friend keep a promise. People read it and nodded. They know which friend. They know which kind of promise. They bought lemon bars and a banned book and said nothing cruel. It felt like breath.

I stood behind the counter and rang a sale and let the drawer shut on its soft rails. Outside a gull shouted at a truck because that is what gulls do when grease goes past on two wheels. Peppermint pounced on a sliver of sunlight and missed, then pretended it was a dignified step. The bell swung. The air moved. Asa walked the far side of the street with the tote and the jacket and a stride that said the day was in hand for the next hour at least.

Martin called a lawyer. We have a cup and a strip and a jacket and a paper. We have a cat who sits in the right place. We have enough for the next step. That is all a shop can ask.

CHAPTER 14

Ledger Audit

The counter is my map table. When the room gets noisy, I clear a square, pull the ledger, and return to what the ink says. Today the noise has a body in it. Harold is gone. People drift in a slow tide. The bell gives smaller notes. I keep my hands steady.

Rafi slid the donation ledger to me with both palms under it so the spine would not twist. He set it in the chalked rectangle we use for any book that needs a chain. Donna clicked the door latch to the customer side so no one would lean in with a curious elbow. Paula stood at the corner with a face like a good teacher ready to keep the rowdy table from eating the test.

I flipped to the page with Harold's morning pledge. The first line is Rafi's neat block print, amount, pledge match, his initials. Below it sits the add-on, new and tidy, gel line smooth as a luxury ad. The words parent advisory fund change the direction of Harold's gift with no authority. The hand is not Rafi's. The ink sits on the paper in a fuller trench, not a ballpoint groove. The pen glides heavy when you use a gel, leaves a tiny lip where the line ends. I set a loupe on the loop of the y and saw a perfect bead sitting at the tail, still glossy in the center. Fresh enough to reflect the task light in a pinprick.

"Photograph first," I said.

Rafi took the shot with the ruler card flat to the page, then two detail frames with the loupe perched at the margin so a stranger could see why a person would argue about instruments. I wrote the time. 1:47. Then I turned the book toward the dome camera in the ceiling and let it sit one beat so the overhead would catch the spread for its own record.

Asa stepped in from the alley and did not break the room's shape. He knows how to enter a shop without making people huddle. He used his eyes before his mouth and went straight to the ledger.

"Start at the tape, not at the ink," he said.

He points us to the wall monitor by the pastry case. The dome camera feeds there when we need it. I keep it off most days because the shop likes to forget it is always observed. Today the shop needs the truth more than comfort.

Rafi put one finger on the monitor's lower bezel to keep himself from tapping the glass like a piano. He scrubbed back on the timeline to twelve twenty and set a marker. He scrubbed to twelve thirty and set another. He toggled the grid so we could jump minute by minute. Camera 1 looks down on the counter from above, fisheye flattened by the software into a neat rectangle. Camera 2 watches the door. Camera 3 watches the banned table. Camera 4 watches the alley tent. Camera 1 is the only one that knows how pens move.

He split the screen and pulled Camera 1 full. The minute bar blipped red at twelve twenty six when the tent camera heard the shout. You cannot hear audio from the dome, but you can watch bodies react. Donna's head snaps. Paula turns. I am already moving. Rafi steps out from behind the counter with the phone in his hand. The ledger sits square in its chalk box at the register edge, open to the pledge line. The jar glints beside it.

"Play," I said.

He let the seconds roll. People surge toward the alley. The

counter stands empty with the ledger like a raft. Two customers linger. Then one man enters from frame right, moves his hand to the edge of the book, and slides the ledger closer to him. He does not lift it. He does not flip pages. He draws it to the lip of the counter as if he wants to write with his elbows free.

"Freeze," I said.

Rafi froze the frame. Zoomed. The hand sits flat to the board, fingers wide. A band gleams on the ring finger. Right hand. The light hits the metal and throws a small spear of white toward the jar. The glint is small, even so it reads as clear as a bell on a cold day.

Rafi wears no jewelry at work. He hates rings near steam. His hands were pouring tea at twelve twenty three and dialing at twelve twenty six. His ring finger is bare. I know this because I watch his knuckles when he pulls a shot and I have a small brain that keeps small facts alive. The camera does not care who I know. It shows me a right hand with a band and a wrist bone that sits under a dark jacket sleeve. The thread pattern at the cuff is pinstripe fine.

Rafi stepped back and let us see the full frame. In the top right corner you can make out the reflection of the pastry case glass, just enough to show the shape of a shoulder. The body facing the ledger stands at the customer side, slightly turned to the right, weight on the left heel. The head is out of frame. The hand is enough.

"Advance three seconds," Asa said.

Rafi tapped. The hand picked up a pen and pulled the book a finger closer. I looked at the pen. The cap glints clear. The body squats, thick. A gel barrel, not our blue house ballpoint. He writes four words without a pause, line even, no hesitation in the down strokes. He dots nothing. He draws a small flourish on the d of advisory because it feels good to him to curve. He drags the pen one inch to the side and sets it on the counter with the cap off. He pushes his palm back and slides the book two inches back into the chalk box like a person with habits about order.

"Freeze," I said again.

Rafi froze. I brought the loupe to the screen in a stupid ritual my brain insists on. You cannot loupe a monitor but it helps me look. The band reflects a rectangle of light. The cuff fabric reads as light gray with a thin dark stripe. I can see the edge of the wrist bone. You cannot learn a man from a bone unless you already know him. I know the jacket. I smelled it at the dry cleaner twenty minutes ago. I watched Asa carry it up my stairs. Pinstripe switched hangers for me and the paper shoulder guard crinkled. The knit at the cuff has a small pull two threads wide. The camera saw that pull and gave it back to me.

"Tag the time," Asa said.

"12:29:42," Rafi said, and wrote it in the margin of my notebook. He grabbed a still and assigned it a number. F1. Hand at ledger, band visible. Pen in hand. He grabbed a second still three seconds later. F2. You can see the pen stroke rising at the end of fund. He grabbed a third still one second later when the hand lifted and the pen lay on the wood, cap off, barrel clear. F3. We stacked the stills at the edge of the counter where the chalk fades. I like a row of truth you can point to.

"Zoom the pen," I said.

Rafi did, and the barrel clicked into a grainy block. Clear body, black gel core. You could call it five brands and be wrong about none. Or you could check the number on our shelf label and match it to the receipt I pulled an hour ago. Yesterday at 3:18, one gel pen sold with a paperback. Loyalty card name on the receipt: Keene, Martin. POS shows SKU 746-GL20-BK. That SKU ties to the gel pen in our spinner rack, row three, hook two. Not the bulk ballpoints in the drawer. I do not have to guess. I can scan the blister pack and watch the register blink the same digits.

"Break the page," I said.

Rafi split the screen. On the right he put the lens over the ledger with the add-on. On the left he held the still of the pen on the counter. The line weight of the add-on sits exactly like a GL20 at slow speed. The stroke maintains fullness even when the hand lifts at the tail. The bead at the y tail reflects the overhead in a pin dot that reads white against black. Our gel pack leaves that bead on cheap paper. The ledger is better paper, so the bead sits clean. We sell a lot of things to a lot of people. It still helps to remember moments when a casual purchase turns into a beacon.

Paula leaned in far enough to see without casting a shadow. "Your ballpoints dig," she said. "You can feel the groove through the back leaf. This sits on top like frosting. No groove."

"Page back," I said.

Rafi lifted the ledger's previous page and set a sheet of dark paper under the leaf to make any indent proud. We side lit with the task lamp at a low angle. The groove of Rafi's pledge line reads like plowed ground. The gel add-on does not ghost. You can flip the page over and run a finger and the paper sits smooth as a cat's back. Ballpoint pushes a trench. Gel puts paint on a wall.

"Play forward ten seconds," Asa said.

Rafi rolled tape. The hand lets go. The person shifts weight, pivots a fraction as if to turn toward the door, then stops because two mothers from the bake tent step in and link arms in front of him in a human gate. They do not see him. Their faces aim at each other, mouths moving. He waits one heartbeat, then slips left past the periodicals display, pen still on the counter. He does not take the pen with him. He does not cap it. He lets the ink dry in air. I can hear Rafi hiss through his teeth for the pen, not for the man. Pens die from that casual neglect.

"Back three seconds," I said. "Freeze."

We froze on the moment his pocket brush passed the spine of the ledger. If you zoom deep, you can see the fabric pull at the inner seam where the liner meets the shell. It is the same spot Angie touched with her nail and said sticky. It is the same crease I swabbed on my desk. The camera is not a lab. It just shows the crease.

"Print these four stills," Asa said to Rafi.

Rafi sent F1 through F4 to the docket printer in the office with the template that auto stamps time and camera number in a bar under the photo. He wrote the capture time and his initials on the back of each. Paula watched his pen and did not correct his angle because she trusts him to write legible when it counts.

I took the ledger and slid a thin plastic sheet between the add-on line and the previous entry so my notes would not transfer oil to the page. I used a pencil, not a pen, because I am not an idiot. I wrote three words at the bottom. gel line added. Then I wrote 12:29:42 camera 1, right hand, ring. I initialed and closed the book. I did not lock it. I set it low behind the cash till where a person would have to reach past Donna to touch it.

"Bring up the receipt," Asa said.

Rafi flipped the monitor from cameras to register, punched in the date and the loyalty card name, and pulled the line for the gel pen and the paperback. He tilted the screen and then printed the receipt copy. It spat from the small printer with a curl. He flattened it with his palm. SKU, time, partial card number, clerk initials. His. He filed the strip in a sleeve and labeled it POS 746-GL20-BK, 3:18 yesterday, Keene.

"Put the pen tray up here," I said.

Donna brought the spinner rack and let me pick a GL20 from the second hook. Clear barrel. Black gel core. Medium point. You can buy it anywhere. Today it came from me. I set it on the counter near the ledger at the same angle as in the still and shot a frame with the ruler card and the house light on full. I never want to argue about which pen point left which line. That argument eats hours and respect. If I can spare us, I do.

"Cut the moment with who else touched the counter," Asa said.

Rafi scrubbed back and forward five minutes and tagged three other hands that brushed the ledger's edge. None slid it. None picked up a pen. One woman blocked the camera when she leaned for a napkin. You can see the top of her head and the shape of her bun, nothing else. She moved fast. The man we care about moved smooth.

Paula pointed with her chin at the jar. "No one reached into the jar while the book sat near the edge," she said. "No fingers. No bills turned. People looked and then ran."

"Frame that," I said, because if we show a jury a slick move near money, they will let the wrong feeling climb in. The jar stood untouched. The theft here is not cash. It is consent.

The door opened on a gust of perfume that has introduced arguments since school board meetings were held in gyms with bad chairs. Nina came in hard, chin up, a phone case with roses in her left hand and a new white folder in her right. She saw the monitor, saw the stills fanned at the edge of my chalk square, saw the ledger behind the till, and swerved toward us like a small boat catching a wake.

"You cannot hide this," she said, too bright. "Sunlight is cleansing. People want to know what happened. Show the tape. The public has a right."

"The public has a lot," I said. "Evidence is not one."

She planted at the end of the counter and set her folder down hard enough to make the pen in it jump. "You think you are the only person who cares about records," she said. "I am here to protect children from seeing filth while they buy cookies. A man died in your alley under a tent you set up. I am asking for transparency. Show me the video."

Paula cocked her head. "You want to show a collapse on a screen at a till," she said. "To whom. The seven year old who wants a cat sticker. The teacher who has to stand at the board at three. The teenager who finally saved eight dollars for a book his father hates. Or do you want to watch it yourself because a steady shot of someone else's loss gives you a feeling you like."

Nina flushed and reached for the folder like a shield. "Do not twist my concern into something lurid," she said.

"You asked me to project a fall," I said. "I am saying no. If you want to file a request with Asa's office, you can. If you want to see the ledger, you cannot. Not today. Not now. This is evidence. I will not let a rumor sit in the footprint of a pen."

She pulled her phone up. "Then I will tell people you are hiding things," she said, aim toward Sylvie's feed, tone for the clip.

"You have already done that," I said. "It did not help Harold. It will not help you."

Asa did not change his face. He placed one palm on the counter in front of the ledger's chalk square and spoke like a man telling a driver to slow for a turn without raising his voice.

"Ms. Carrow," he said, "we do not release footage in a shop for browsers to pick at with their thumbs. We log it. We move it to a server. We cut the minutes that matter. The family sees first if the family wants. The court sees when the court is ready. You can stand here and act loud. You cannot make me hand you a tape. If you have a question that belongs to motive and deeds, you can ask it in the council chamber at the right time."

She took a breath that turned into a laugh with no humor in it. "You get off on this," she said to me. "You like being the gate."

"I like being exact," I said. "We have a tape that shows a hand. We have a band. We have a pen. We have a register line. We have a dry cleaner tag. That is a lot. I do not need to feed you the seconds it took to write four words."

Her eyes flicked to the stills and then back to my face. "Whose hand," she said. "Say it. Just say it. People will find out anyway."

"I am not a feed," I said. "You can read the paper when it prints a record. Today you can buy a muffin or go home."

Rafi slid the stills into sleeves and stacked them under the counter. He does not argue with people who want a scene. He makes scenes smaller by removing stage props. Paula pulled the banned table placard three inches to the left so Nina would have to step around it to keep shouting. It is a trick she learned in school hallways. Move the obstacle so the current shifts.

Nina tried one more swing. "I know about your display and your donor and your ledger tricks," she said. "I saw the new line. I am not blind."

"Good eye," I said. "Bad interpretation." I put the ledger in a flat box and slid the lid on with both palms so the cardboard would sigh and close. I wrote the time on the tape I crossed over the seam. I signed my name across the tape. I set the box low behind the till again and placed my hand on it until I felt the pulse in my wrist slow.

"Leave," Donna said, gentle but final. She can clear a room without wrecking a day. It is a gift.

Nina lifted her folder and made a sound that wanted to be a scoff and ended up a throat clear. She did not want to give us a clip of herself being told no. She settled for a photo of the banned table sign at a cruel angle and a caption that would get her immediate likes. She went for the door with a hand that shook enough to tell her she should have stayed home.

Asa waited until the bell stopped quivering. "Back to it," he said.

Rafi returned the counter to its square shape and pulled the camera feed back to full. He scrubbed to twelve thirty one and let us watch the rest of the minute. People jostled. A child cried and was scooped. A plate tipped and was caught. The pen, cap off, lay next to the ledger until Donna reached over with a napkin and put the cap back on with two fingers. The napkin is in the bag by the sink now with other small facts no one respects until they need one.

"Print the ledger page," I said.

He made a flatbed scan with the small office machine that has seen more pamphlets than it deserves. He put the copy in a sleeve marked copy for report. He closed the lid on the ledger box, lifted the box, and carried it into the office with the slow dignity of a man carrying a cake that cannot shake.

I called Angie and told her the scarf lifted and that she is a star. I told her we would pick it up at four and that I would bring her the cookies she likes, the ones with the almond dust she calls dangerous. I said dangerous out loud and watched the room measure the word. Paula smiled for the first time in an hour. It did not last. It did not need to.

We pulled the register log for the minutes after the collapse and tagged the exact time the drawer closed on a donation Rafi recorded as a match from Harold's friend, a woman with eyes like a winter sky who handed me a bill without looking at it. We set her kindness on the page next to a false line and felt the scales tilt where they belong.

Asa stepped into the office, checked the lock, and returned with the small seal we use when we send anything to his server. He put the drive on the counter, slid the files, verified the hash, and wrote the code on his card with the kind of care a person usually saves for names. He handed me nothing. He put the drive in his coat and zipped the pocket so I would not have to watch him carry it. I am more human than I like to admit about certain objects.

Nina stood outside on the sidewalk and talked to Sylvie's camera about children and harm while holding a coffee she bought from the cart up the street. The line on her cup matched no line in my shop. She glanced at the window, saw me not looking at her, and raised her voice. The town walked by her the way water slides around a piling. She will get her likes. She will not get my tape.

"Close the book," I said, and I did. I set my hands on the box one more time and felt its weight. Evidence is paper with a spine. You keep it where sunlight cannot warp it. You bring it out when a door you respect asks for it. The rest of the world can wait.

CHAPTER 15

Donor Past

Council files age in two ways. Some grow soft at the corners from honest hands, others harden into boxes no one opens unless someone like me insists. The clerk's office keeps both kinds. It smells like pencil shavings and old toner. The window fan ticks. The clock above the copy fee sign runs two minutes slow, which is funny only if you do not run a shop where time stamps matter.

Paula signed the visitor sheet in neat black, then nodded at the counter. "Records, please. Donations to the town from the Keene family, last fifteen years. Also any liaison memos regarding a program called Advisory Fund."

The clerk on today, Marisol, had the calm of a person unbothered by other people's urgency. She flipped a binder to the K tab, slid a finger down a column, and said she would bring two cartons from the mezzanine and one binder from under the case. Her voice stayed mild when she added that Advisory Fund did ring a bell.

"Cart or table," she asked.

"Cart," Paula said. "Flat bed, not wire. These pages shed."

Marisol grinned. "Spoken like a librarian," she said, and returned with a blue cart and a ring of keys. She unlocked a half door and let us pass into the shallow records room. The lights came up hard and clean. One wall of bankers boxes, one wall of metal shelving with binders, one scanner with a temper. No magic, which suits me.

I set my notebook down, rolled my shoulders once, and pulled on gloves. Paula did the same. Marisol set the two Keene cartons on the cart and the binder on top, then parked us by a wide table and left us with the fan and the clock.

"Chain," I said out loud, more for me than the room.

Paula wrote the carton numbers, shelf code, our names, the time. She always writes like the paper might be called to testify. It is a habit I trust. She opened the first carton. Inside: file folders with the slow confidence of money that travels in envelopes. Naming tab after naming tab. Youth Reading Week. Plaza benches. Two clocks for the council chamber, which do not run in sync. A handful of general gifts with the kind of cover letters that make town managers smile and then scan.

The second carton carried heavier files. Legal counsel packets stapled as if the staples were meant to stay forever. A glossy press kit from another town. Harbor name on the folder top, but the photographs were not our streets. A hotel ballroom, a podium, a navy backdrop that said Harbor Region Advisory Fund across a field of logos. The first page inside framed a timeline and a gift amount. The four pages after that told a story in careful language about partnership and youth and listening. None of that would matter if the rest of the file did not whisper why.

Paula lifted a stapled packet that had crumpled at the corner long ago. She slid it under the task lamp and read the subject line. Inquiry Regarding Safety Incident, Harbor Region, Five Years Prior. She scanned the first page, then handed it to me without commentary the way professionals pass a scalpel.

The gist: a Keene company contracted with the region on a facilities project. A serious incident led to settlements and hearings. Tempers ran high. The company released statements. Community leaders asked for structural changes. Soon after, a new gift appeared. The Advisory Fund cuffed around several programs. Reading rooms. Youth mentors. A hotline line item. A press conference photo showed a familiar profile at a podium with the word Advisory over his shoulder, the R cropped by a microphone stand. The caption named him, not Harold. Martin Keene, in a tie the color of a bruise, with a smile that knew how to wait until a flash fired. The photographer caught the sign behind him, big letters printed on foam board in a simple sans serif. Advisory Fund. Same phrase as today's gel line in my ledger, one extra word in the add-on to make it sound town-honest: parent advisory fund.

"Photograph," I said.

We did. Full page with the caption, then the crop: Martin's tie, the edge of the board, the word Advisory boxed by the field of logos. I set my small ruler at the bottom and took the shot with my phone, then with Paula's, then with the office scanner that takes a second try to wake up and then behaves like a workhorse.

Paula pulled out the binder Marisol had added to our stack. Council Minutes, Selected Subcommittees. She flipped to a section marked Special Calls. Her thumb eased under a plastic sleeve and she popped open a three-hole spine to free a packet. Someone long ago had tucked an insert behind it. A memo on creamy paper, thinner than the rest, like a personal letter that later got folded into official record.

I read the header. Communications Draft, board prep, typed names at the bottom, then a line that was not typed: Advisory Fund phrasing preferred, underlined twice in a hand I had seen on a note before. The loops climbed shallow. The downstrokes leaned right, not cute, not sloppy. The ink looked like gel because it sat on the fibers without any trench. The tail on the y had a tiny bead at its tip. Paula did not need to say it. We were both looking at the same thing.

"Compare," Paula said, and pulled an old folder from the first carton with a note Martin had scrawled on a seating chart for a donor lunch. He had added Please put Advisory Fund on podium sign, use line weight three, and had initialed MK without flourish. Same slanted hand. Same tail beads. Same neat upward flick at the d when he felt good about a line. He had used the phrase as a brand long before today's ledger tried to corral Harold's pledge.

I took out my loupe and set it over the y in Advisory on the memo. The bead glinted under the task lamp. Not fountain. Not ballpoint. Gel. The handwriting had aged very little between the old note and last week's letter we had scanned for another request. Same slope. Same pressure. People can disguise their voice in a letter, not their rhythm.

Paula slid the memo into a sleeve and wrote a citation on a small card: Minutes binder 2, tab 14, insert page with handwritten line in MK's hand. She writes like a person who expects a judge to ask where a thing sat on a shelf. I admire her for that.

"Why this phrase," I said, not because I needed the English, but because motive likes its own music. "Why is he so faithful to it."

Paula pulled her glasses down one notch and gave me that look my grandmother used to give me when I asked for cinnamon rolls before noon. "Because it sounds neutral," she said. "Because it sounds involving. Who can argue with advice. It suggests care without promising action. It puts the giver in the chair with the microphone and the community under the header. And because he invented it for a shame that needed plaster. Men like to repeat themselves when the spell worked once."

Her tone was dry and precise. My hands itched to do something petty, like pull the staples out of a glossy with my nails. I did not. I looked back at the photo of Martin at the microphone and pictured last night's dinner rehearsal in his head. Insert gift, introduce advisory panel, aim floodlight away from what the last advisory paper covered over. Then this morning we set a table in my shop with a frame of books that make people read, and Harold, with his neat cuffs and his open face, praised the display with his tea cup in hand and thanked me for letting him put his name under the match. The one story outshouted the other. Martin's brand shuddered. He wrote an add-on line and poured something bitter into a cup and walked a blazer down Harbor Avenue sixteen minutes after a man fell in my tent.

Marisol came back with a small smile and a heavy binder the color of a bruise. "Found one more thing," she said. "Clippings. Our intern scanned last year and we kept the originals because people like to touch paper."

She set it next to the cartons and opened to a section marked Harbor Region, five years ago. The first clipping was a press release, all smooth edges. The second from a daily in the city had a paragraph near the middle about the company's safety performance and an op-ed under it that asked why advisory panels show up only after the press conference is over. The third showed a podium with that foam board again, the same lettering, the same word in bold. The photo credit was a stringer with a sharp eye. In this frame the photographer had stepped to one side and captured Martin's hand on the edge of the podium, thumb tapping the board like a metronome.

I took the scan, then closed the binder gently and set it to the side. Clues are quieter than rants. These would do.

"Check the council chamber minutes," Paula said. "If Harbor Region used the same boilerplate here when they announced the plaza benches, his language might have bled into our record. People copy the words they hear most."

We checked. A press release from two years ago for the benches had banners and cupcakes. The mayor at the time had printed remarks. At the bottom of the page: Thanks to the Keene Family Advisory Fund. Our town did not have one. The gift named it into being for the space of a sentence and then the town used the phrase as if it had always existed. We took the scan.

Paula pulled the minutes for the night the library board reviewed donor restrictions. A typed paragraph flagged that strings would not be allowed to influence selection. In the margin, handwriting in the same tidy slope offered alternate language: advisory panels exist to represent community voice. The phrase hummed like a hymn. In the lower right corner, the initials MK. There it was, not loud, but plain. He had been in the room. He had lobbying privileges that make my teeth hurt. He wrote on our minutes like he was helping. In some rooms maybe he did. In this one, today, he did not.

"Photograph the margin," I said.

We took the shot with a macro so the pen tip bead would read. The dot at the end of the word voice sat like a small planet above a horizon. Gel again, smooth, recent for that year. Same brand family as yesterday's purchase in my register. People stay with the tools they like.

Marisol peeked back in. "Need the microfilm reader," she asked. "The Herald's archive has a better shot of that podium. The board shows the font well."

"Yes," Paula said.

"I will set it up," Marisol said. "The machine eats film if you walk away. Stand guard."

We followed her around the counter into the small newspaper nook where a tired reader sat on a table like a television from the first apartment you ever rented. Marisol threaded a spool with practiced fingers and spun forward to the date in the margin. The screen glowed blue, then gray, then black while letters found their edges. The frame on the page showed the podium with clean light, the board high behind the mic. Advisory Fund repeated in the same line weight across the middle. Martin's head filled the left third. The reporter had angled the lens so that the words lined up behind him like a halo.

"Print," I said.

The reader clicked and spat a warm copy that smelled faintly of wet paper. I slid my ruler to the right of the words and shot the print with my phone. Then I positioned my gel pen photo from the register next to it, the clear barrel catching the same kind of shine, and took the frame that proves nothing by itself and everything in a line.

Paula shook her head, not at the man, at the habit. "He never learned how to cede the microphone," she said. "He thinks process ends with his speech."

"Today the speech ran into a table full of books," I said.

"Today his phrase tried to crawl into your ledger," she said. "Same thought. Same need for control."

I opened my notebook and wrote: Advisory Fund, prior scandal, Harbor Region. Phrase repeated in old minutes in MK hand. Photo shows MK at podium with board. Same language on benches presser. Ledger add-on repeats phrase with parent tacked on. I underlined parent not because the word changed anything, but because it made the town lean a certain way. He knew that. He counted on it.

Paula pulled one more file from the first carton. It held a letter on heavy stock with Harold's name at the top, not Martin's. A thank you note from the library for a past gift. Two lines down, a handwritten postscript in a different hand than the typed signature: Let's keep this about books, not optics. That was Harold's cursive. Loose. Open. It bumped into the right margin like a person who hates fences. The letter was three years old. Harold had been pushing for a shelf that made readers breathe different air. Today he got it, and raised a cup to it, and then fell on my asphalt.

"Copy that," Paula said, and her voice roughened. She loved Harold like the town loves a man who gives without asking for his name larger than the event title.

We copied the note, sleeve sealed, citation card tucked behind it. We put the original back in its folder and slid the folder into the carton with care. We closed the cartons and wrote a short chain of what we touched. Marisol reappeared with her keys as if summoned by paper itself.

"Done," she said.

"For now," Paula said. "We will cite these when we need to speak in a room with microphones."

Marisol checked our pages, initialed the scan log, and nodded at the blue cart. "Take the binder with you if the deputy signs," she said. "He has a deposit account for it. We charge nothing for grief."

"Thank you," I said.

Outside, the sun had shifted, which mattered only because the photo on my phone looked truer in slant light. I stopped on the steps and framed the screen with my fingers to check the focus on the word Advisory. A woman paused with a stroller to let me finish. She did not ask what I was photographing. People who live in small towns know when a person is making sure a thing exists in two places.

Back in the shop, the bell sang a clean note. Rafi had filled the water jugs, and Donna had reset the pastry case. Paula set our binder behind the register and asked for the staff stool. She sat, opened to the margin where the MK hand lived, and breathed out slow.

"Say it," I said.

"Advisory Fund, in his hand," she said. "Matches line weight, matches slope, matches MK initials. The phrase appears in our board minutes from three years ago. He wrote it into the margin like a suggestion. The council later echoed it in a release. The same phrase shows on the Harbor Region podium sign. He has used it for years to frame donations when a story needs to change shape."

I let her voice land. It does more than mine in rooms that doubt booksellers.

"Will you say that under oath," I asked, quiet.

"I will," she said. "I will also explain why words are never neutral when a donor writes them on government paper."

I slid the binder into a rigid sleeve and taped it like a newborn. Peppermint jumped up, sniffed the plastic, and decided it did not interest him. He hopped down again and went to sleep on the mat by the door like a guard who knows the next shift will ask for his whiskers.

Paula tapped the binder once as if giving it courage. "Root motive," she said. "His narrative. He guards it with money and phrases that sound kind. Your display cracked it in plain daylight. He tried to steer the afternoon with a line in a ledger and a cup."

I wrote one card for the file in block letters that do not favor anyone's brand. Advisory Fund, MK's phrase, used here and there, carries the same work as today's add-on. The phrase itself is not a crime. The way it moved through our paper is the map.

The door opened and a woman came in for a paperback she had on hold. Paula smiled and rang her up and slid a tote across the counter. I slid the binder behind the till and placed my hand on it for one slow breath. Then I took it away and went to make tea for a man with red eyes who needed to sit by the window and look at the harbor.

We had our root. We had the photo of the board. We had the line in his hand. We had enough to show why a person who loved control would do a thing that would break a room. The next part would be ugly. I prefer ugly that lives on paper to ugly that runs loose.

CHAPTER 16

Spouse Pressure

The back office was ready before he arrived. I like rooms to be honest. One table, three chairs, a fixed camera in the ceiling corner, a red dot lit, a card freshly slid into its slot. The blinds were down, the task lamp set to noon white, the sound of the fan low and steady. Rafi had taped blue corners on the floor where each chair should sit so the camera angle would not change when nerves did. The ledger copy sat in a rigid sleeve. The register receipt lay on a clipboard. Two photo sleeves showed the green test squares beside today's paper. The bagged cup and saucer rested in a tray like sleeping animals. I set my notebook open to a fresh page and wrote the hour at the top. Small things make a day hold still.

Asa checked the camera light and nodded once. He keeps his coat open when a conversation might need breathing room. He tested the door latch, then leaned on the file cabinet with the kind of quiet that steadies a table. He and the cabinet understand gravity in the same way.

Martin stepped in exactly on his body's version of time. He wore the cardigan he keeps for church panels, warm and careful, as if knit could soften concrete. He saw the camera. His smile clocked it and tried to turn it into a friend. He took the seat with the painter's tape marks at its feet, then adjusted the chair a finger's width, because men like him always move something when a room asks them to hold still. Asa stayed by the file cabinet, quiet as furniture until a law needed a voice.

"I appreciate the privacy," Martin said, not looking at the lens. "This is upsetting. I would like to frame it in the most helpful way for the town."

"Then we will start with the three items that are not feelings," I said. "The receipt for the gel pen you bought here yesterday at three eighteen. The copy of the ledger page you touched at twelve twenty nine. The photos of the green shift from the cup rim and your blazer pocket. The camera is recording. You know how to talk in straight lines. Let us use that."

He glanced toward the wall shelf where the jug and paper cups sit. He did not ask. He placed his hands on the table like a student ready to recite. The skin around his eyes looked tired in a human way. The set of his mouth was not human. It was trained.

"Everyone buys pens," he said lightly. "I might have bought one for my wife. I buy from you often. I am on your loyalty list."

"You bought a clear barrel gel with a medium tip," I said. "SKU ending in GL20. You carried it out in a bag with a paperback, a romance with a pink spine. You used the same brand to write four words on my ledger while the counter was empty. We have the still. The dome caught your right hand, your cuff, and your ring."

He did not look at the still. He looked at me. I set the receipt above the ledger copy so the numbers spoke to each other without me explaining their friendship.

"Nina stirred your book," he said. "I saw her on a live clip telling people you keep sloppy entries. She said the club would fix that. She is not subtle about what she dislikes."

"She was loud," I said. "She did not touch the ledger. The only hand that slid the book to the edge and picked up a clear barrel was yours. We can go frame by frame if you want to stand under the camera while we narrate."

He shifted in the chair one inch. The blue tape under his feet kept the rest honest. He moved to the next stone with the same ease he uses when a donor misses a rehearsal cue and he needs to carry a speech across a gap.

"Bria had motive," he said. "She wanted her pastry ribbon and that crowd. She asked Harold about his toast time yesterday. She was right by the cups. She could have mixed a sample wrong. It happens every year. I read recall notices. One bad ingredient and we all pretend it is no one's fault because we like her smile."

"She was running sales at the minute," I said. "Her lids stayed sealed. The footage shows both her hands. She never left her square. The tent cups came from her box, one set, plain glaze, even stain line. The cup Harold used was not from that set."

"Then the club woman," he said. "She frothed for that reporter. She does not need poison to do harm. She needed a moment. I saw her bag. It was large and black and lined with intent."

"If you want to stand up and point at the fixed camera and argue that noise changes chemistry, go ahead," I said. "She did not pour. Her pen is a fine nib. She did not buy our gel. She touched paper and volume only."

He folded his hands and unfolded them. He took a breath the way people take a step when they walk into cold surf. He tried the sentence he had packed for the moment he thought would come, the sentence he believed would sound like contrition in the right voice.

"Then it was me," he said. "A mistake. I reached to help. I straightened a cup on the tray, it looked wrong on the angle, and it must have been one you meant to rinse. I moved it toward Harold because he was right there with his toast. I regret that. I regret a lot today."

The phrase landed like a thumbprint across fresh polish. Straightened a cup on the tray. Not adjusted, not fixed, not swapped. Straightened. The way a person who lied about a courier sticker said she straightened a label when she had peeled and set it again. The rhythm was a rehearsal.

"The tent cups were fine," I said. "The crooked one lived by my espresso bar for months. Rafi washed it yesterday. The glaze shows crazing in a starburst you can see under a lamp. The stain line sits higher than the tent cups. The saucer chipped and went into lost and found. The set never left the building until a hand with your ring carried one piece out. That tray did not give it to Harold. You did."

He sat quiet for three beats. I let them pass. The fixed camera recorded the stillness, which is as useful as speech when the case goes from my table to the court's.

"My reputation is not a hobby," he said finally. "I am not a fox in the coop. I do not sneak."

"You do not sneak," I agreed. "You draft, you dress, you rehearse. When a word will serve you, you make it a sign. When a phrase will move a room, you put it on a podium. When a ledger can redirect a pledge, you write a line that sounds civic and takes control. When a cup is in your way, you straighten it."

He flushed. He looked at the copy of the page with the add-on. He did not touch it. He adjusted his cuff. I slid the photo of the green strip across the table, the one shot beside today's paper. The square glowed cool. He glanced down, made a small sound in his throat, and looked away. People always want the picture to be a metaphor. It is a chemical shift and a timestamp, nothing more. That is enough.

"Our cleaner swabbed the pocket lip of your blazer," I said. "You checked it in at twelve forty two. We got there and did the first test at twelve fifty two. We did the cup rim strip in this office with the masthead in the frame. Both strips turned the same green. I ran a control on a clean ramekin. It stayed white. I filmed my hands. The card in the camera was new."

"You run a cafe," he said. "There are odd cleaners in a cafe. A jug of something lives under every sink in this town. You sell romance. You love a story."

"We love proof," I said. "Ask Asa who has to stand up in a court where stories go to take a nap."

Asa did not move. He is a lesson in weight. He has spent years turning noise into paragraphs a jury can read without help.

Martin tried the softer route again. People like him can pull mercy from a rock when they want it. He lowered his voice and aimed for the lens without looking at it.

"I am not a villain," he said. "I am a spouse who has kept a lot of pieces in the air for a long time. Harold liked to throw new pieces up and ask me to clap. He liked to draw attention. I preferred to build rooms where the minutes do not eat people alive. You set a table that asked for a fight. I tried to guide it."

"You tried to steer a pledge," I said. "Your add-on uses a phrase you have pushed for years. We pulled council minutes and found it in your hand. We pulled clippings and found you at a podium beside the same words. You wrote that line under Rafi's entry to take control of a match that was not yours. Then you touched a cup."

He breathed through his nose again, long, a small whistle inaudible except to people who sit at many tables with men like him. He looked at Asa.

"Do you have enough," he asked. "Or is this still a neighbor talk where we let the tape run and test how I sound."

"We have the items we have," Asa said. "We will ask you to come to the station for a recorded interview. You can bring counsel. You can say your piece. You can keep your peace. We are not here to bargain. We are here so this shop can get back to being a shop."

"Then let me say one thing for the record," Martin said, sitting straighter. "I did not mean harm. I saw a tray. I saw a crooked cup. I straightened it. If that begins to look like intent, you are seeing shapes on the wall that are not there."

"You bought a gel," I said. "You wrote a line. You touched a cup that did not belong on that tray. You dropped a jacket at a cleaner during the window and it carried the same bitter trace as the cup rim. Those are shapes. They are not shadows."

He aimed for outrage, then measured it and set the volume lower.

"You put books in the window that ask for trouble," he said. "You positioned a table for a fight. Do you feel nothing about what you lit."

"I feel a lot," I said. "I feel a man's hand in mine as he put his name next to our match. I feel a town that can hold more than one idea in its head. I feel a person who could not let that happen without his thumb on the page. That is why we are sitting here."

He put both palms flat on the table. The camera caught the small tremor in one finger. He stared at the ledger copy as if eye contact could melt ink. He tried the last small lie he had saved, the one he hoped would stitch the morning back together enough to let him sleep tonight.

"I straightened a cup on the tray," he said, softer, as if quiet could make the words truer.

"You planted a cup," I said. "You planted a line. You planted a jacket at a counter with a rush ticket. You wanted the day to move around your edits."

He closed his eyes. He opened them. He set his jaw. He let the trained smile die for a moment, and the man under it looked older and less balanced. He looked at the shelf again. The jug and the paper cups sat like props.

"Water," he said.

"No," I said.

Asa stepped from the cabinet and opened the door. He did not touch Martin's shoulder. He did not rush him. He did not slow him. He stood to one side the way a good usher stands when the aisle needs to be clear.

"We will meet you at the station," Asa said. "Bring your counsel if you want. There will be a cooler in the hall."

Martin rose. He took one last look at the ledger sleeve and the green squares. He aimed a sentence at me like a dart that hoped to stick to anything soft and keep it from falling.

"You do not have to hate me," he said.

"I do not," I said. "I will not carry your story for you."

He nodded as if we had agreed on seating for a gala. He stepped out. The red light stayed on until the door latch clicked, then I reached up and stopped the card. I wrote one line at the top of my page. He used straightened when he meant planted. Then I closed the notebook and breathed into my hands once, because I still own a body.

Paula slipped in from the stair as if she had never left the hall. She handed Asa a sheet from the minutes binder and touched the ledger box with her knuckles like a blessing. Rafi set two cups on the shelf and did not pour. He knows the difference between kindness and theater. The fan hummed. The room held.

"Will he talk at the station," Paula asked.

"He will talk around himself until his lawyer talks about risk," I said. "The word he picked for himself today is the tell."

"Straightened," she said.

"Straightened," I said. "The same shelter a sticker liar builds for a corner lift. He wants the verbs to wear manners."

Asa nodded once, then left with the binder and the photo sleeves in a flat bag. The bell downstairs gave a small note that none of us followed. I cleared the table, put the sleeves back into their box, and wiped the line where his fingers had rested. Dawn had felt simple. Noon had grown fangs. The next hour would belong to rooms where forms live. I turned the camera off and turned myself back toward the counter where words behave.

I pulled the card from the camera, labeled the sleeve with time and room, and set it beside the ledger box. Habit is a handrail. I wrote a chain sticker for each piece on the table and pressed the edges down with my thumb so the glue would hold. Date, hour, initials. I keep the same block letters I used on library slips when I was sixteen. Precision looks humble in pencil. It still works.

The phone on the shelf buzzed twice. Angie had sent a text from the counter at Pinstripe. She wrote, Jacket sent with Deputy, pocket lip still tacky, told him about rush, told him about smell, thanks for the cookies. I sent back a heart and a thank you and the time that would live in the log. She does not ask for anything else. She will, later, ask for a novel with a happy ending. I will give her one and a coupon.

Donna knocked with two knuckles and stuck in her head. Her voice stayed low. "Two reporters," she said. "One from the Herald, one from the school blog. Do you want to give them a sentence that will keep them from eating the windows."

"Tell them the shop is cooperating," I said. "Tell them we are closed for an hour. No names. No drama. If they use a kind photo of Harold from the archive, I will give them a muffin when I come up."

"Copy," she said. She always smiles when she says copy. She never pretends it is clever.

Paula sat in the chair that had been Martin's and adjusted it back to the tape marks. She placed the binder on the table and opened to the minutes where his hand sat in the margin. She read the line out loud, not for me, for the air. Advisory panels exist to represent community voice. The period was tiny and square. The tail on the y carried the same bead as today's add-on. She placed the sheet beside the ledger copy so a stranger could see how ink behaves when one person holds a pen for years.

Rafi came back with a small bin and pointed toward the sink. "All tea from the urn is in the drain," he said. "I wiped the valve and the rim. New liners. New jugs. I kept the spoon that sat next to the tent tray. It has no stain, but I bagged it."

"You can teach a class," Paula said.

"I will when I stop shaking," he said, and made a face that was honest and quick.

Peppermint slipped under the chair and leaped into the empty cardboard box the sleeves had come in. He turned once, lay down, and thumped his tail. The camera was off. He is not a prop. I scratched his chin and he closed his eyes with the calm of a thing that expects the room to right itself.

My phone chimed. Sylvie again. She wanted a quote that would fit under a photo and travel. I wrote, We honor Harold with clean facts. The rest waits for the deputy. She responded with a thumbs up that will soon sit under a caption I cannot control. Fine. We will outlast captions.

Asa came back for the drive, slid it into a padded mailer, and wrote the number of the case across the flap with a fat marker. He does not like thin pens. They lie in court. Thick ink reads true from the last row. He asked for the ledger box. I handed it over with the ruler and the stickers. He lifted it with both hands as if weight should still be respected when the lid is only cardboard.

"Anything you forgot to say," he asked me, not looking up.

"I said enough," I said. "He showed what he needed to show."

"Good," he said. "I like it when people pick their own words."

The room felt wider after he left. Paula closed the binder and set it upright against the wall, then wrote a small card for its pocket with the page numbers we would need later. Rafi wiped the table again with a cloth he keeps for the office, one that never goes near the bar. He set the cloth in a zip bag and put it in the bin. He does not like loose ends.

I opened my notebook and wrote a list I could read cold on a bad day. Receipt, gel. Ledger, add-on. Cup, glaze. Saucer, chip. Blazer, pocket. Strip, green. Cleaner, time. Minutes, phrase. Photo, board. Voice, straightened. The list looked small, which comforted me. Big cases get lost in scrolls. This one fits in a hand.

"Do you want water," Paula asked me.

"Yes," I said, and took my own paper cup from the shelf. It tasted like the back room and dust and a town that was trying to be better than yesterday. I drank the whole thing and threw the cup away and washed my hands.

"Ready," she asked.

"Ready," I said, and put the sleeves back into the tote in the order that would make sense to the next pair of eyes.

CHAPTER 17

Confrontation

Interview Room B is all tile, clock, and table. No posters. No comfort. The camera light blinks red in the corner. Asa sets a yellow pad down and keeps his hands clear of the tape line that marks the evidence zone. I sit to his left with the chain: sleeves, photos, ledger copy, the gel-pen receipt, the cleaner's slip, and two printed stills from our overhead camera. The bagged cup rides in a foam cradle like it matters, because it does.

Martin takes the chair that faces the lens. He knows where to look. He gives it a quick glance, then keeps his eyes on Asa. He wore the church cardigan again. No pinstripe today. He has a lawyer two doors down who asked for five minutes, took seven, and left him with a plan that depends on tone. Asa gives him no tone to push against.

"State your name for the record," Asa says.

"Martin Keene."

"Spell your last name."

"K E E N E."

"Do you understand you are being recorded."

"I do."

"Do you want water."

"No."

He wants control. He starts with a steady breath. "I want to help," he says.

"Good," Asa says, and nods at me. I slide Exhibit A into the light.

"Exhibit A," I say, because we are past the point where casual helps. "Cup from the alley tent. Porcelain. Internal stain line higher than the set used in the tent. Under loupe, glaze shows a unique starburst pattern. This cup has lived by our espresso bar for months, not in Bria's box. The saucer with the matching chip was in our lost-and-found bin last night. We bagged both."

I set the loupe photo beside the cup so the crazing reads in a clean ring. I do not lecture. I do not need to. Martin tilts his head toward the screen and then away, like a man trying not to blink during an eye test.

"Exhibit B," Asa says, sliding the next sleeve. "Register receipt. Yesterday at 3:18 p.m., Peppermint Cat Bookshop sold one gel pen, clear barrel, medium tip, SKU ending GL20, along with a paperback. Loyalty account shows buyer name as Martin Keene."

Martin says nothing. His lawyer has told him a receipt is not a confession. That is fine. We are not here to let one item pull the weight of five.

"Exhibit C," I say, laying down the ledger copy with the ruler card printed in the margin. "Donation ledger page. First entry in Rafi's hand reflects Harold's pledge and match. At 12:29:42 today, during the alley response, our overhead camera recorded a right hand with a wedding band sliding the ledger toward the edge, picking up a clear-barrel gel pen, and writing an add-on line that moves Harold's pledge to a 'parent advisory fund.' The hand then set the pen down, cap off, and slid the book back into the chalk box. The stills are time stamped. Camera 1. We printed the frames."

Asa places the stills side by side. In one you can see the ring. In the next you can see the pen. I watch Martin's eyes land on the small glint at the cuff and then jump to the corner of the table as if the glint might burn him.

"Exhibit D," Asa says. "Dry cleaner slip from Pinstripe, logged at 12:42 p.m. today. Item described as 'men's blazer.' Clerk noted tack on inner pocket lip and a faint bitter odor. She bagged and held the garment. We collected it, swabbed the pocket lip, and obtained a green shift on a field strip. We repeated the test. We photographed both strips next to today's masthead and a ruler card. Control on clean porcelain stayed white. That sits in the lab queue now. The preliminary match is plain."

I put the photo with the green square under the lamp and let the color speak. I do not list the compound. I do not need to. Asa nods again.

"Exhibit E," I say, because you do not skip the piece that clears the loud suspect when you are closing a loop. "Square reader export from the bake tent at 12:26 p.m. shows Bria Leduc running two sales during the exact window of the pour and fall. Video from the tent shows her at the table with both hands full, lids still sealed on her trays. No pour. No reach."

Asa folds his hands. "We are going to let you speak," he says to Martin. "But we will not let you wander. Start with noon. Tell me where your hands were from 11:55 to 12:35."

Martin looks at the table rather than the light. "Helping," he says. "Greeting people. Picking up litter. Straightening a cup on the tray. I admit that. I thought a guest had set it down off center and it would spill. I moved it closer to the center. If that cup was the one you are holding, then I made a mistake."

He landed on the verb he liked in the back office. He repeats it like it can turn a plant into an accident. I keep my face quiet.

"You 'straightened a cup on the tray,'" Asa repeats. He does not smile. "Which tray."

"The one at the tent edge," Martin says. "The one with the mixed cups."

"There were no mixed cups at the tent," I say. "You are describing the shop's overflow tray by our bar. The tent cups were plain and even. The tray sat inside the tent lip, not at the edge. The crooked cup came from the bar."

He tries again. "Someone set one on the wrong tray. It happens. Those events get messy."

"You set it on the wrong tray," I say. "Your right hand took it to Harold. We have the path on camera. We have the time. We have the Square gap where Bria is tied up with two sales and not pouring. We have an audio spike from a phone near the shelf at 12:00:06."

He pivots. "You cannot prove intent. Not mine. Not anyone's. A cup is a cup. A crowded tent is chaos."

Asa slides the cleaner's receipt closer without pushing. "You dropped a blazer with tack on the pocket lip at 12:42," he says. "You asked for a rush. You said you spilled something. You handed them a jacket from the shoulder like you did not want your fingers near the mouth. Our clerk swabbed and called. We did the rest."

Martin lifts his chin. "I dropped it because it was sticky," he says. "I did not examine the stick. You run a shop. You know how sugar gum feels."

"You do not get a green field strip from sugar," I say. "And sugar does not ride a lip like that."

He goes quiet. Asa lets the air sit for five seconds. Silence is not a trick. It is a tool.

"We do not have to like the word intent," Asa says after the pause. "We only have to stack the objects until they hold up. You bought a gel pen. When Harold fell and the room broke into noise, you wrote a line that would have moved his pledge to a phrase you favor. We pulled minutes that show you wrote that phrase into council paper in the past. We pulled a photo of you at a podium with the same phrase on a board. The pen you like leaves a bead at the tail. It left a bead on our ledger. It left a bead on a margin three years ago. That is one stack."

He taps the next exhibit. "You touched a cup that does not belong in the tent set. It carries a unique crazing pattern you can spot under a task lamp. The saucer with the matching chip was in our bin last night. The stain line inside the cup sits higher than the tent cups. That is two."

He taps the photo. "Your blazer pocket lip carries the same bitter trace we lifted from the cup rim. We shot both strips next to today's masthead. Control stayed white. That is three."

He nods at the stills. "Your right hand with your ring slid the ledger to the edge, wrote the line, and set the pen down uncapped. The register says you bought the gel. Rafi's hand is bare. He was in the alley. That is four."

He glances at the Square export. "Bria's device log ties her to sales in the exact minute. Video shows lids on her trays. That is five."

He looks up and holds Martin's gaze. "You can keep this in the key of accident. No one at this table will sing along."

Martin folds his fingers together and unlaces them. The trained smile tries to surface and dies at the corner. He works the soft angle again, the one designed to slide past resistance.

"I did not mean to hurt Harold," he says. "I meant to stop him. He wanted to attach his name to your display and throw more money at a table that inflames people. He kept putting himself in front of cameras and letting the town tear itself in half over a stack of books, and then he pledged a match to make himself the hero of an argument that never ends. I wanted to embarrass him. I wanted him to stop. I wanted him to drink a bitter sip and spit and sit down like a man who had been told no."

"You poured something into a cup that could kill," I say. "You carried it. You handed it to him. That is not a prank."

He flinches like I hit him. I did not raise my voice. I do not need to.

"I did not pour," he says.

"You handled a jacket with the residue," Asa says. "You handled the cup. You handled the ledger. Your story has you in every important place with a different verb for each. Help. Straighten. Move. Show. The camera and the strips do not care what you call your hand."

He looks at the dot on the camera and at the mirrored glass and at the door and back at me. He wants me to give him a soft landing. I do not have one for him. He is the kind of man who confuses neat language with clean acts. He has had decades of practice. Today his verbs lost their cover.

"Why the ledger," I ask, not because I need a motive to finish the chain, but because I want the record to show the thing he tried to do with paper.

He answers like a man who thinks the right sentence can still make a room nod. "Because if Harold's money went to a parent advisory fund, it would cool the room. People listen to that phrase. They relax. It sounds like process. It shifts a fight out of a shop and into meetings. I tried to move the heat."

"And the cup," I say.

His eyes flick back to the exhibit, to the starburst in the glaze. When he speaks, the sentence comes out smaller. "He is a showman," he says. "He makes the room bend around his kindness. He was going to toast your table like a martyr. I wanted him to choke on the moment and think."

"You got the choke," Asa says. "You got the floor. You will not like how the room heard it."

Martin presses his palms to the edge of the table. "I did not know," he says. "I thought it would be a quick lesson. A bitter wash. A face. A cough. Not this."

I look at the cleaner's strip again. The green square sits calm and blank. It does not care about regret.

"You had options," I say. "You could have argued on the record. You could have spoken in council. You could have written a letter and signed it. You could have left the tent and let the town decide if it wants to read on a Saturday. You picked a cup and a pen."

He tries one more redirect, a smaller one. "Nina played her part," he says. "She climbed on her box and made this worse. Bria set a field. Paula pushed an archive. Harold brought his name."

"Everyone brought something," Asa says. "Only one of you brought a bitter to a tea tent."

Martin's face changes like a tide line. The practiced muscles let go first, then the jaw. The shoulders drop last. He looks older.

"I meant to embarrass him," he says. "I wanted the pledge to land where it would feel safe and dull. I wanted him to stay home next time."

"No one buys that," I say. "Not as a shield. You know what you put in contact with his mouth. You know it is not a spice."

He looks at his hands. "I did not pour," he says again, quieter.

Asa leans back a fraction, then speaks in the voice he uses when he is done letting a person try on versions of themselves.

"Here is what happens next," he says. "We move this file across the hall. We log the items you have seen into evidence. We send the strips to the lab and get the full spec. We take a sworn statement from the cleaner. We attach your receipt, the stills, the ledger copy, the Square export, the loupe photos, and the council minutes where you wrote your phrase into a margin. We note your words about embarrassment. We note your phrase 'straightened a cup.' We do not argue motive. We present the chain."

Martin nods, then shakes his head, then nods again. The lawyer opens the door on the other side of the glass and steps in. He sits, sets his pen on the pad, and touches his client's sleeve like a metronome.

"We will stop here," the lawyer says.

"We have what we need," Asa says.

I gather the sleeves and stack them in order. Crazed cup. Saucer chip. Gel receipt. Ledger copy with stills. Cleaner slip. Strip photos next to the masthead. Square export. I tape the bundle and sign across the seam. I do not look at Martin. He had my attention for hours. He used it on edits.

Asa reads the formal close for the camera. Date. Time. Room. Names. The red light stops. The clock ticks. The tile can breathe again.

In the hall, the air is cooler. Paula sits on the bench with her binder closed on her knees. Rafi stands with two paper cups and gives one to me. I drink. It tastes like water. It tastes like the hour.

"Did he say it," Paula asks.

"He said embarrassment," I say.

Paula nods once. "He would."

"Lab will give us the rest," Asa says. "We have the chain."

Across the hall, Sylvie lowers her phone when she sees my face and lets the live slot pass to a photo of the harbor. Outside the station door, the bell in the square gives one slow note. Not for ceremony. For time.

CHAPTER 18

Arrest

The station lobby holds sound like a bowl holds water. Voices enter, cool against tile and glass, then settle. A kid whispers near a brochure rack. A copy machine ticks. The front desk light hums. The clock above the property window shows 4:03. I sit on a bench that has held grieving people and bored ones in equal measure and keep my hands on my bag so I do not shred a tissue into thread.

Paula sits to my right with the binder across her knees. She slid a sticky flag at the page where Advisory Fund lives in Martin's hand. She has closed the cover now, both palms flat to keep the thing calm. Rafi is next to her with paper cups he has not touched. He gives me a small nod every few minutes like a metronome. He does not try to talk me into calm. He knows the room does not need speech from us.

Asa steps through the swing gate with a file under his arm and the look he wears when work is about to get formal. He speaks to the sergeant at the front desk. He signs a line. He waits for the inner door to release with a buzz and a click. The charge sheet leaves his hand and lands with a weight that feels heavier than paper. A second later, the side door opens and Martin walks in with a deputy at each elbow.

No cuffs in the lobby. This town avoids spectacle where it can. He wears the cardigan again and the same careful shoes he wore at a council photo four months back. The lawyer from the interview sits in the corner with his bag open and a tablet glowing. He says nothing. He lets his client read the room and pick a mask.

Martin chooses polite. Of course he does. He keeps his chin level and his eyes on the desk, not on the small cluster of people to his left, not on the young officer who will hold a phone while he signs forms. He does not look at me. I did not expect him to. I do not need anything from his face.

The front desk officer runs through the intake script. Name. Address. Birth date. He repeats the charges once, slow, no flourish. Tampering. Fraud. Homicide. He assigns the case number that will live on every slip and form from now on. He speaks the number twice. The numbers echo off tile and sit next to the clock like they plan to stay until the paint fades.

"Property," the sergeant says.

Martin places his wallet on the tray. Phone. Keys. A pen that is not a gel. A metal clip. The officer reads each item aloud for the microphone the desk keeps low and stubborn. He slips the phone into a bag with a barcode and seals it while the camera above the window watches. He opens a drawer and pulls a paper envelope, prints the case number on the flap, folds, staples, and sets it in a bin. He moves slow. Stations teach slow. Slow wins in rooms where speed breeds error.

"Shoes," the sergeant says.

Martin bends and unlaces. The deputy runs a wand over the soles, checks the arch, nods, and slides the shoes back across the mat. Martin puts them on without hurry. The clock clicks to 4:07.

"Do you understand the charges as read," Asa asks him across the counter.

"I do," Martin says.

"Do you want to make a statement right now," Asa asks.

"My attorney advises I wait," Martin says.

"You can call when we move you to the back," Asa says. "You may not use that phone to contact witnesses."

Martin does not nod. He does not argue. He signs the property card with a ballpoint that drags rather than a gel that glides. The small trench the pen leaves in the receipt makes me feel more grounded than I want to admit. The officer tears the carbon and lays his copy in a tray that has seen decades of hands.

The inner door buzzes again. A deputy opens it. Martin walks through. He does not look back. The door shuts and the lobby deepens in quiet.

Now the station turns to the hangers-on.

Nina is here. She stands near the brochures with a file folder pressed to her chest and the air of a person who does not feel the rule against phones is about her. She moves closer to the desk as if she were rehearsing her next clip. One hand goes up to shape a sentence that is not yet spoken. The front desk officer clocks the hand, reads the posture, and keeps his voice calm.

"No filming in the lobby," he says. "No livestreams. If you need a statement, ask for the PIO and wait on the steps."

Nina hears the words. She does not accept them. She raises the phone anyway. Asa does not raise his voice. He walks to the edge of the tape line and stands with his hands behind his back in the posture of a person who has been taught where a room ends.

"Ms. Carrow," he says. "Put the phone away."

She tries to talk through him. "The town needs answers," she says. "Donors are dead in alleys while librarians shove filth at children."

She is talking to the ceiling camera now and the inside of her own skull. The lobby does not clap. Paula's face does not move. Rafi folds his arms and looks at the exit.

"Phone," Asa says again.

"I am press," she says.

"You are not press," he says. "You are a person with a phone. Put it away or accept a citation and step outside."

"You cannot silence concern," she says. "You cannot silence a mother."

"You came here for a scene," I say before she can wind herself higher. "You can make it outside where the steps like noise."

She swings her eyes to me. There is heat there. There is a need for fuel the room will not provide.

"Ms. Carrow," the sergeant says now, patient but finished, "walk out or take the paper."

She holds for one more breath and then flips the phone down into her bag with a sharp motion that a different person would feel silly about later. She plants her feet like she plans to give one more line and Asa lifts a hand and lowers it in the simple gesture teachers use when they want a class to sit. He writes on a pad, tears a slip, and hands it to the desk. The desk officer fills in a block, stamps a corner with the station seal, and holds the paper through the window.

"Disorderly conduct, lobby," the officer says. "Court date at the bottom, printed, not handwritten. Your signature is not an admission. It is a promise to show up."

Nina stares at the paper like it will morph into a commendation if she breathes on it hard enough. It does not. She signs with a quick jerk of her pen and huffs air through her nose like an angry horse. She pivots toward the door and grazes the edge of the brochure rack with her shoulder. A trifold slides to the floor. She leaves it there because that is on brand for her. Donna would have picked it up. Paula does. She replaces it without comment. She is better at being human than I am today.

Bria arrives on the back of that small storm. Her hair is pinned up with a butter knife she probably grabbed when she set her last tray. Her apron is clean now. She wears a cardigan that is not hers. The cuffs reach past her hands. The Square reader dangles out of her bag like she could sell a scone to the clerk while she waits. She stops at the threshold, checks the posted sign about phones, slides her own into a pocket without a fuss, and looks for a face to explain the world.

Rafi stands and opens his arms in the universal figure eight of a hug you can step into or not. Bria steps in. She is small when she cries. She keeps the sound low and dry. I hold her shoulder until her breath stops chasing itself.

"I did not touch a pot," she says. "I did not even pour water. I held a lid and a reader, and then a man fell and a boy dropped a tray of brownies and I stepped wrong and said a word my mother hates."

"You were on the log," I say. "The video is clean. Your lids were sealed. Your day was honest."

She nods and looks at me like I control the air and could spare her some. I do not. I can do something smaller. I can say the one line she needs.

"I am sorry you were dragged," I say. "I am sorry you were in that tent when the worst part happened. You worked like a clock today. You fed people. You did not hurt anyone. You deserve a ribbon and a nap."

Her mouth bumps into a smile that does not hold. She wipes her face with a sleeve that is too long and gives a small laugh when the cuff flops. She catches the cuff with her other hand and holds it in place like a doll mother saving her child from tripping.

Asa steps over. He does not touch her until she moves first. She steps toward him like a person who accepts that not all men in coats bevel edges with their mouths.

"Ms. Leduc," he says. "We cleared your name from the tent timeline. I will say so out loud. In front of the room."

He turns to the lobby and lifts his voice one notch. He does not boom. He lets the tiles carry his sentence.

"For anyone here who is still building a story in their head," he says, "Ms. Leduc did not pour. Her device log shows two sales at the exact minute. The video shows her hands. She has no part in the cup. She gets an apology from this office for rumors we cannot control."

It is not a long speech. It is the right one. It fills the space where a whisper was trying to grow. A man near the rack nods. A woman who posted once today without thinking lowers her eyes to the floor. Sylvie, who is sitting near the door with her phone in a case, writes without lifting her head. She is not filming. She is taking notes like a reporter who wants the sentence right.

"Thank you," Bria says. "I still have trays to wash."

"Go," I say. "Rafi will walk you to the back. Use our sink. Use our kettle. Leave the tent bins to me."

Rafi takes her arm and moves like a tug turning a ship at low speed. He knows how to read sorrow that needs to stay moving. They step into the late sun and I watch her shoulders drop one inch. You could miss it if you were a person who thinks drama is loud. The good news today will be quiet.

The inner door opens again. A deputy brings out a plastic tray of personal effects to hand to Martin's lawyer for the initial sign-off. The lawyer slides a copy of the charge sheet back across the counter to Asa with a note about voluntary appearance and bonds. Asa takes the paper and reads it in the way he reads breakfast menus. He writes a number in the margin and circles it. He does not haggle. He gives the clerk the figure and asks for the schedule that will go to the judge's inbox. The station printer whirs into life and spits out a form with a barcode that looks like a train yard.

Paula leans toward me. "He will be out on bond," she says, not upset, not surprised. "Process is process."

"I know," I say. "I still want the lock of a door to say something to him."

"It did," she says. "It said no."

Nina returns. Of course she does. She stands outside the glass and records herself. Her mouth works as if she were biting down on a lemon you are required to watch. The glass cuts the sound. I am grateful for glass. A teenager with a skateboard leans on his grip tape and watches her on his phone while he watches her through the window. He looks bored. That is the best we can hope for. Boredom turns most fires to ash if you let it.

Sylvie stands. She smooths her skirt and approaches the desk like a person who would like to speak where speaking is allowed. The front desk officer tips his chin. She offers her card.

"One line for the record," she says to Asa. "Not a quote that bleeds. A sentence that holds."

Asa nods. He gives her the same thing he gave Bria, shaped for the page.

"The investigation moved from rumor to record," he says. "We are booking Martin Keene on charges tied to the ledger add-on, the cup, and the residue. A second party is cited for disorderly conduct at the shop and here. The bake vendor received a public apology and is clear."

Sylvie writes without looking up. She asks one more.

"Name the second party," she says.

"Nina Carrow," he says.

"Thank you," she says. "I have no taste for grandstanding today."

"You do not most days," I say.

She half smiles. "Write me a sidebar later," she says. "What a ledger means to a shop. People do not know."

"I will," I say. "No adjectives."

"No adjectives," she says, and steps back to her bench to file a lean story that will live online in a half hour and in print tomorrow above the weather. She will not use photos of Harold before the coroner calls the family. She will not post the clip of the fall. She will post a still of the table with the books in their upright peace. She will leave room for the rest of the town to breathe tonight.

The booking officer calls the next name. A boy with a stupid grin steps up to pay a traffic citation. The lobby remembers how to be the place where small things happen. The big thing has moved through. It leaves a trail of paper and heat.

The side door opens and Mae steps in. Her hair is set the way it is set for council nights. She looks at me and then at the desk. She speaks to Asa with clean vowels.

"Status," she says.

"Booked," he says. "The lab will add spec to the strip. The clerk has the charges."

She nods and turns to me. "The display stays," she says. "Any attempt to pull it will run through a meeting. We are not doing that tonight."

"Thank you," I say.

She does not smile. She sets her bag down and signs a form the clerk slides toward her. She supports procedure even when she wants to burn down a comment thread. It is one of the ten reasons people keep voting for her.

The door from the hallway opens and Paula's counterpart from the library board steps in with a stack of paper that already looks like a shield. She sees Paula's binder and relaxes two notches. These two have planned enough book drives together to know when the other has the document that matters. They exchange four words and a nod, then sit. The town runs on small trust you can see from across a room.

A low sound carries from the inner hall. Not drama. A cough. A chair leg. The whirr of a machine that sits where the public cannot watch. I do not stand to see. My part is done in this room. My part will pick up again in my shop when I hang a small sign on the banned table that says Context matters and put the ledger in a safe and make biscuits because people will need starch and butter to keep from crying.

The sergeant hands Asa the last sheet. Asa signs. He puts the pen in his pocket. He turns to the lobby and speaks the room back to itself.

"Folks," he says, "we are done here for now."

He does not clap his hands. He does not herd. He lets quiet settle over tile. People stand or sit. Those who came for flesh leave. Those who came to be seen have had their minute and do not know where to put their hands now. Paula closes the binder and passes it to me. I slip it into a rigid sleeve and hold the edge like a thing that might jump.

Bria returns with Rafi through the side door that leads to the alley. She has washed her face. She has a bakery towel over her shoulder like a flag for a country I would live in. He has flour on his sleeve again. Flour is better than bile.

"You ready," he asks me.

"Yes," I say.

"Wait," Asa says.

He walks with us to the steps so the camera above the door will record our faces for the timestamp that will later answer a question in a room with no windows. Outside, the square holds late light. The bell gives a note that feathered out on the first ring. A breeze moves stale heat off the street and replaces it with air that does not hate lungs.

At the top of the steps he stops us with one line. "Two things," he says. "One. lock the gel rack. No more sales until I sign off. Two. tell Donna to expect a record request from the city desk. We will cut the minute we need and give them no more."

"Copy," I say.

"Copy," Rafi echoes.

Mae comes out behind us and sees a cluster on the grass that is about to turn into a circle around Nina's phone. She steps off the stairs and crosses the lawn with a speed that would scare a cat. She slides between the phone and the first woman who wants to talk into it. She says something only that woman can hear. The woman laughs in surprise and steps back. Mae hands Nina her own citation sheet with a look that says, you invited this, and turns away before Nina can set a hook.

Bria squeezes my hand once and goes toward the alley with Rafi. They will pass the coffee cart. He will buy her a seltzer because bubbles help. She will try to pay and he will look offended and then accept half a dollar because pride needs something to do. They will go through the gate and he will hold it open with his foot because his hands will be carrying her bins. I know this because we have done days together that were not murder days and some parts of a town keep their shape.

Paula tucks the binder under her arm and waits with me on the top step. She watches Sylvie finish her story. She watches the skateboard kid flick his board to his hand and hook it under his arm like a briefcase. She watches two council aides cross the square with a tray of coffees and a posture that says they have paperwork that needs signatures and a boss who will walk out to the curb if she has to.

"Clean story," Paula says after a beat.

I follow her gaze to Sylvie. She has set the headline in a font that does not shout. She has used a period instead of an exclamation point. She has added one quote from Asa and one line from me. She has typed Harold's name without the adjectives the comments will try to paste on him. She will run his photo tomorrow from the day he held a book about tides and try not to cry when she sets the caption.

"Clean," I say. "No grandstanding."

Sylvie looks up and catches my eye and tips her phone toward me like a toast with no drink. She sends the file. The screen flashes and then returns to her notes app, where she has written a list that begins with Names, spelling. She will sleep tonight. She learns to. Or she quits. She has not quit yet.

Mae's phone rings. She listens. She says yes and no in equal measure. She pockets it and turns to me.

"Council at seven," she says. "We will issue a steady line. No pull of your display. No nonsense at public comment. Bring Paula if she wants to speak as a librarian, not as a litigant."

"I will be there," Paula says.

I nod. I do not want a podium. I will sit in a row with my hands on my bag and watch a line of townspeople tell the room who they are. I will let the bell do the talking when it is time.

Asa goes back in. The door shuts on the hum of the lobby and a printer that has not finished eating its day. I stand on the steps and let the light sit on my face for a minute. I have to return to my counter. I have to hang a sign that says we are closed for an hour and sweep under a table because flour does not care about grief. I will move the banned books three inches deeper on the table so the angry miss fewer spines. I will brew a pot and make sure the water line on the machine is clean and clear. I will not delete the phone messages from people who picked a side for sport. I will let them sit until morning. I will give the blazer back to Asa when the lab calls. I will put the chipped saucer in the box with the cup and the ledger scans and I will label the entire thing with a card in my block print that says Cup pattern links to pour. Ledger line links to phrase. Residue ties hand to lip. Finished.

Paula touches my elbow. "Walk," she says.

We take the square slow and then the street. We do not talk much. We pass the flower shop and the closed sign at the yarn place where the owner once told me she prefers storm days for sales because knitters buy wool when wind taps glass. We pass the shoe repair where a pair of boots stares out of the window like a dog that wants a walk. We pass three houses with flags that wave as if any fabric knows anything about honor.

At the corner I hear the small voice of a boy ask his mother if the book table is still there. She says yes and no at once. Yes, the table is there. No, we are not going in right now. He takes this with more grace than any adult did today.

We cut down the alley. The tent frame is still up. The cloth walls are down and folded. The grass has pressed marks where chairs sat. The air here smells like sugar and metal. Rafi has already hosed the corner where the worst moment landed. I do not see bleach. I see clean water and the path it left as it found the drain.

Peppermint trots from the back door with a leaf in his mouth like a prize. He drops it at my shoe and looks up, not for praise, but to see if I am the person he remembers. I scratch the top of his head and he blinks and leans and then walks past me like the king who has noted his subject and moves on to other tasks. I did not know I needed that.

Inside the shop, Donna has turned the open sign to sorry and set a tray of cups on the back counter for washing. She has mopped once with clean water and marked the wet spots with a sign that asks people not to slip. She has set the banned table to rights with the placards square and the spines facing the door in a way that looks like an invitation rather than a dare.

She looks up at me with the kind of face you only get from staff who have done the exact day you needed them to do while you were away catching a man with paper. I touch her forearm. She nods. We speak a small language that does not need vowels. I go to the office and put the binder in the safe. I go to the counter and place the ledger box next to the scale we use for packages and write the word logged across the tape. I open the cash till and put a note in the drawer for the morning that says count matches night and a small box next to it that holds a chocolate I will hand to Rafi when he comes up the stairs.

The bell rings once as the front door opens on a gust. It is not a customer. It is the bell doing what bells do in this town when a day returns to itself. I let the note fade and then wipe the counter with a clean cloth and the citrus bottle that will always smell like this chapter. I set the bottle down and write one card for the box on the top shelf. Arrest recorded. Citation issued. Apology given. Story filed. Display stays.

On the steps outside, the skateboard kid flips his board again and lands on the bolts with the certainty of a person who owns one thing that keeps agreeing with his feet. I choose to take that as a sign. Not a grand one. A small one I can hold. I lock the door for the hour we promised the station and set the timer on the espresso machine so it will not sleep. I line the cups in a row that looks like a parade of moons. I feed the cat. I sit on the stool behind the till, breathe in through my nose, out through my mouth, and plan how to tell the book club next week that we now have two more rules pinned to the cork board by the clock. No off network devices. No secret funds.

Sylvie's story pings my phone. The headline reads: Shop Ledger and Cup Test Lead to Arrest in Bake Tent Death. No exclamation marks. No ghoulish clip. A photo of the table with Peppermint's tail in the corner where he snuck into the frame like a comma. She uses Asa's line. She uses mine. She ends with one sentence that turns the day into a thing the town can fold and put in a pocket. The investigation left rumor behind. Clean records carried it home.

I set the phone face down and look at the room until it looks like my room again. Then I pull the stool forward, reach for a pen, and write the board for tonight's council line so I will not say the wrong word when the microphone blinks at me. I will say, we keep the display. I will say, we log gifts with precision. I will say, a ledger is not a theater. I will sit down.

The clock in the corner clicks to 5:01. The square outside breathes. The station across town has new names on sheets and new entries on drives. The cleaning crew will pull a bag from a bin that smells like coffee and paper and something darker. Nina will post a clip that gets her the numbers she wants from the people she wants them from. It will not change the card I wrote for the box on the top shelf. Peppermint will nap on the shipping scale. Rafi will wash a pan with the concentration of a monk. Paula will iron a blouse and drink tea that is not bitter and practice the line that contains the word advisory without letting it own her mouth.

I pick up the bell clapper and tap the brass light, soft. One clean note crosses the shop and finds its seat.

CHAPTER 19

Community Reset

We opened at six for the meeting we promised, lights warm, windows cracked, coffee already poured. The shop felt like itself again, paper and citrus and the faint clean smell of a floor that was rinsed twice after a bad hour. The banned table stayed where it belonged, front and center. I added a simple sign on foam board and clipped it to a stand.

Context for Readers

Each book here has been challenged somewhere. We shelve it with a short note about why it matters. Parents choose for their own kids. No one chooses for everyone.

No italics. No flames. You could read it and breathe at the same time.

Chairs went out in a circle, not rows. Circles turn heat into talk. Rafi set extra cups by the pump pot, then tucked the bell rope through his fingers and gave it a quiet test that did not carry. Donna laid pencils and index cards on a tray for people who ask better questions when they write first. Paula stood by the table with the binder tucked under her arm and a smile that knows how to keep a room level. Peppermint trotted a patrol around the legs, tail up, and chose a seat under the plant by the cooking shelf where he could watch both the door and the counter.

By six ten we had thirty people. Teachers, a pair of high schoolers with summer jobs, two moms who always shop together on Thursdays, the mail carrier on his way home, Mae in a plain blazer with her hair pinned up sparse. No cameras. Sylvie took a chair with a small notebook, not the phone. Nina was not here. That helped the oxygen.

I welcomed them, short. No sermon. "We lost a neighbor," I said. "We kept the ledger clean. The table stays. Tonight is for clarity. Ask. Listen. Sleep better."

Paula started with three minutes that fit in a pocket. She explained what a challenge is and what it is not. She explained that librarians build collections to serve a whole town, not one house. She explained that our display mirrors what her field has had to hold for decades. No drama. She anchors rooms with verbs like serve, document, preserve. People leaned forward without reaching for phones.

Then Q and A. No microphone, no speeches. One person at a time, clear questions, clear answers. I kept the stack with a raised hand and a nod. It felt like a book club that had put away cookies and picked up backbone.

First up, Mr. Harper from the frame shop, who pretends to be gruff until you watch him brush dust from a gilded edge. "What happens to money when it shows up on a day like this," he asked, chin toward the ledger box under the counter.

"It gets logged as pledged first," I said. "Then as received, with a note about where the giver wants it to land. If the request violates law or policy, the gift declines or returns. No one rewrites the line to hijack intent. We will post our donation rules on the corkboard so it is not guesswork."

Paula nodded. "The library holds the same line. Restricted gifts are a contract, not a mood. We will publish our policy again this week. You can print it and stick it on your fridge."

Mrs. Alvarez, fifth grade teacher, asked if students would see this display on field trips. "No," I said. "Field trips get a shelf pull we curate with you. This table is for the public. Teachers set context for their classes. Parents set context at home. We set a context for the shop. That is three circles, not one circle that eats the others."

A senior from the high school raised a hand, Cheyenne, who once shelved romances here in exchange for store credit. "Can I suggest titles for the notes," she asked. "I can write why a book helped me when my cousin came out."

"You can," I said. "Stick a card in the jar. We will ask your permission before we post your words. First names only. No online crosspost without consent."

A man with a beard I know from yard sales cleared his throat. "Who decides what sits on that table," he asked. "Because I saw one book that makes my blood crawl, but I saw another that made me feel seen."

"Both can sit," I said. "Some books save a person you will never meet. Some books do not speak to you at all. We do not build a list by comfort. We build a list by record and reach. Paula sets the library's span the same way, with more structure and a board."

Mae leaned in with a short addition. "And if you want to argue a title," she said without flint, "come to council with a sentence that starts with an I, not a they. We will listen. We will not swing cameras at each other."

Donna walked a tray around, collected cards, and passed a few up. One asked if we would ever hide the table during events. "No," I said. "We do not move it for a bake sale, a baby shower pop up, or anything that makes cash register life simple. If you want sugar without spine, the cafe down the block has nice muffins and no strong opinions. You will not hurt my feelings."

They laughed because it was true and because truth was a relief.

Then the hard one. A mom with a toddler on her lap and fear parked behind her eyes. "My daughter is nine," she said. "She reads anything with a cat on the cover. Can I trust that she will not pull something from that table that will take weeks to explain."

"You can trust yourself," I said. "The table has a sign that says ask. Ask me. Ask Paula. Ask your friend who reads two books a week and never forgets a plot twist. We will steer you. We do not herd. And I will help you find ten books with cats on the cover that do not break breakfast. Peppermint will inspect each one."

Peppermint yawned on cue, which let the room exhale.

Paula added, "We also label by age band in the stacks. We do not shelve a book for a college class next to chapter books. If your daughter reads above level, we help you find titles that stretch, not scorch."

Hands again. A shop owner who lives on latte foam and kindness asked what we need. I answered like a cashier. "Three things. Patience while we file forms. Respect for the sign that says no off-network devices. Pledge cards you fill out fully if you plan to give. Full names make the world go. Anonymous cash goes in a receipt envelope with a date. No edits later."

"Do you need volunteers," a man asked from behind the travel shelf.

"Yes," I said. "Greeters for next Saturday, two hours at the door to answer easy questions and point to the sign. Shelf readers on Monday evenings. People who can brew a pot without fear. If you like mopping, I have a bucket that will make you a saint."

They laughed again and five hands went up. Donna wrote names as if catching them kept the town from leaking.

We moved through the cards. Someone wanted us to post the titles with links to reviews that have more light than heat. We will. Someone asked if we had a process to collect challenges that are not a storm at the counter. We do now. A simple form, no tricks. It lives in a clear sleeve by the corkboard. Turn it in and we date it, read it, and answer in writing. No more air fights.

Two teens asked if they could make the context notes into a zine. Paula's smile turned wide in the way you save for bright ideas that do not cost money. "Yes," she said. "Print a small run. Sell it by the register. Keep the profit. Credit sources. Use fonts older than your phone."

A man in a cap asked if we would add a book club for parents who feel lost in this wave. "We will," I said. "Short books first. One meeting a month. Tea, not theatrics. Rafi will bake shortbread. We will call it Reading Room."

From the back a small voice. "Can I pet your cat," the toddler asked.

"After the bell," I said. "He clocks out at the bell."

The binder came out for one short segment. Paula opened to the page that people have not seen, the one that shows the phrase painted across a past podium and written in a margin in a hand that keeps trying to shape this town. She did not name the man. Everyone in the room who reads a paper knew. She explained why a phrase that sounds gentle can bend a policy if you let it. She did not aim it at a throat. She aimed it at a habit.

Then thanks. Neat lines of thanks that Paula can carry to her review like receipts. A teacher: "Your notes made this feel possible." A dad: "Thank you for helping me set a boundary without a fist." A grandma: "You used small words to explain a big mess." Paula wrote them on a single card so they would not feel like she was padding a file. She will tuck the card into her planner and forget it there until a hard meeting needs it.

We closed with ground rules for what lives here after today. I read them out loud and tacked the sheet to the corkboard at adult eye level. No secret ballots. No blackouts. No off-network devices in the circle. Donation edits only by the person who gave the money, in daylight, with initials. Questions welcome. Record requests go through the inbox with dates. If you touch a cup, you rinse it. If you move a chair, you slide it, not sling it.

Mae had one line for the room. "Councils are slow by design," she said. "That is not a flaw. It keeps the temperature down. You want speed, go for a run. You want policy, bring a sentence and sit."

I set a small plate of lemon bars on the counter, made by a baker who had stood in our lobby and heard an apology that mattered. People took one square, not two. The room understood rationing when a day had been heavy.

Peppermint stood, stretched, and jumped up on the banned table. He threaded between spines, then sat square beside the sign and blinked as if to say he had read every page and approved the commas. I lifted him and set him on the counter for the last part.

"Time," I said.

Rafi stepped to the bell and wrapped his hand around the rope. He looked at the table once. He looked at Paula and at me. He looked at the door and the faces we had kept sane for an hour. Then he pulled down and let the clapper find the brass.

One clean note crossed the room and held steady. You could feel it press the air flat, not hard, not sharp, the pitch that says this day is done and this place still belongs to books and to the people who read them. He let the note fade without a second strike. The town stood still for a beat, then chairs brushed floor and hands found plates and conversations dropped to a hum.

I left the bell to swing itself quiet and walked the table once more, fingers on the foam board sign to make sure the clips were tight. The index cards in the jar had doubled. The corkboard had a list of volunteers with phone numbers someone had written slowly so there would be no wrong digits at eight in the morning. Paula slid her thanks card into her planner and closed the cover.

Rafi caught my eye. No words. I nodded. We were not repaired, not cured, not immune. We had swept, brewed, posted, answered. The table stayed. The bell had said enough.

The door breathed. The bell over it lifted, did not ring, fell into stillness again. We watched it like a final line that lands clean and then stops where it should.

CHAPTER 20

Cat and Cups

Closing time came on soft feet. The square had settled, the last mugs were drying on the rack, and the shop wore that late hum I like, a hush with a pulse. Donna flipped the sign to closed and rolled a towel tight for the morning. Rafi stacked chairs two by two, neat as a ledger line. Paula had gone home with her binder and a lemon bar, the kind of balance she deserves.

I opened the safe and pulled the rigid evidence box to the counter. The cup sat in its foam cradle, glaze starburst under the task lamp, the stain line where it always sits. Beside it, the saucer space was empty, a taped outline waiting for a match.

Peppermint nosed the Romance shelf and disappeared behind a drift of paperbacks with sun-kissed couples on the covers. A moment later I heard a light clink, then the deliberate scrape of porcelain across wood. He trotted out with the missing saucer hooked under his chin like a platter too grand for his small jaw. Tail high, eyes pleased, he set it at my toes and meowed once for the record.

"You earn your keep," I said, and he blinked as if to say the staff should try to keep up.

I rinsed the saucer fast under warm water and set it on a clean towel. The chip on the rim was exactly where the loupe had told us it would be, a tiny crescent that matched the twin on the cup lip like two halves of a closed eye. I dabbed it dry and pressed the saucer into its cutout. The fit was exact. Some things do click.

On the counter, I laid out the paper that would ride with the porcelain. First, the ledger page copy that shows Harold's line in Rafi's hand and the add-on below it, the gel bead at the tail of the word fund shining under the lamp. Second, the cleaner slip, time stamped in the window that matters, clerk note about tack on the pocket lip, a service line no one wants to write. Third, the strip photo with the green square, today's masthead broad as proof beside it, no tricks.

I slid each sheet into a sleeve, pressed the air out with the flat of my palm, and stacked them in order, cup to ledger to jacket to strip. Chains are simple when you let them be.

Rafi joined me at the counter and set a fresh label sheet by the box. "Tabs," he said. "If you want to find a word in a hurry later."

"I want the day to sit down," I said. "Tabs help."

He peeled and placed, one clear tab per sleeve, tiny block letters with room to breathe. Cup. Ledger. Cleaner. Strip. He writes like a person who cares about the next set of eyes.

Donna wiped the bell rope and worked the clapper once in a whisper to test the felt we'd added last week. "He had good timing," she said.

"He liked a room," I said. "He would have stayed for the Q and A and brought his own card."

She smiled and finished the tray. The sink hissed a last rinse, then went quiet.

I turned to the small index drawer under the counter, the one that holds our cards for cases, the ones that matter and the ones that only taught us how to watch. The old ones leave dust on my fingers. I like the way that feels. It reminds me that shops are built by hands.

New card, clean corner, the pencil I keep for this only. I printed the line we had earned.

Cup pattern links to pour.
Money tried to steer the story.
The evidence is what held.

I dated the card and added my initials and the hour. Rafi added his. Donna tapped a corner and gave me a look that said the right words matter. I slid the card into the slip on the box lid and pressed the lip until the click sounded like a small door that knows how to close.

Peppermint leaped to the counter and inspected the saucer one more time, nose close, whiskers forward, a formal check. He rubbed his cheek against the box edge, filed it as ours, and sat on the scale with his tail tucked like a cashier after a long shift.

"Bed," Donna told him.

He did not move. Cats ignore orders until the orders sound like their own ideas.

I walked the box to the safe, paused for a second in the doorway, and looked back over the shop. The banned table was set. The sign held steady on its clip. The chairs faced each other, not the door. The corkboard rules were square and clean. The jar of index cards with reader notes for context sat next to a jar of pencils with their points sharpened, no bite marks. The place looked like itself, only smarter.

In the safe, I set the box on the middle shelf, between Box 42B from another life and the file where we keep the worst names quiet until the county says we can speak. I passed a hand over the lid, not a blessing, not superstition. A ritual you build so your bones know what part of the day just ended.

When I came back out, Rafi had written one more card for the corkboard, small, bottom right corner where only the people who care enough to read the whole board will see it.

Thank you to the volunteers who signed up tonight.
We will train you.
We will hand you a towel before we hand you a microphone.

"Copy that," I said.

He shrugged. "We got lucky," he said. "People want to help. Give them a job before they look for a spotlight."

Donna pulled the register tape and counted the till, lips moving once, twice, then she nodded. "Balanced," she said. "Like a table that does not rock."

We turned off the front row of lights. The task lamp stayed on for the last pass. Peppermint hopped down and followed me aisle to aisle while I checked for stray mugs, a forgotten scarf, a book face-down like a sleeper who needs a blanket. In Romance, a stack of paperbacks leaned like a chorus line. I straightened the spines and found a faint ring on the wood where the saucer had slept. I wiped it with a cloth and the ring let go.

"Found your bed," I told the cat. He blinked slow and returned to the counter, where the shipping scale gives his spine a warm flat place. He curled with the care of a thing that knows how to take proper shape.

I washed my hands, the kind of wash that runs past the wrists and asks the day to leave. I dried them on the good towel and hung it on the rack. The clock on the wall over the club board rolled its minute hand to the mark.

"What now," Donna asked.

"Sleep," I said. "Council at seven. We keep the table. We keep the rules. We bring biscuits."

"On it," Rafi said. "Shortbread, edges neat."

He took the compost bucket and stepped out the back. Donna grabbed her bag and waved, that bare-handed motion that trainees always copy because it looks like a shop trick. She locked the staff door behind her. The alley gave a cool exhale. The air in the shop met it and calmed.

I stood at the counter alone for a moment and read the new card on the box again. Cup pattern links to pour. Money tried to steer the story. The evidence is what held. Simple, square, more spine than flourish. I put the pencil back in its slot. I turned the last lamp off.

At the front, I lifted the bell clapper and let it kiss brass once. The note went out across paper and glass, clean and even, and sat in the room like a promise you plan to keep. Peppermint flicked an ear, approved, and closed his eyes.

I locked the door and checked it twice. The square outside had gone to shadow, a soft-edged picture of a small town that has bad days and keeps itself anyway. The window threw my reflection back at me, tired and awake. I do not mind that mix. It is what a shop owner looks like when the ledger is closed and the box is labeled and the cat is asleep on the scale.

I walked home with the smell of citrus on my hands and the bell still inside my bones.

END OF BOOK TWO

PEPPERMINT CAT BOOKSHOP MYSTERIES

ABOUT THE AUTHOR

Ivy Grant is a celebrated fiction author best known for her gripping mysteries and heart-racing adventure novels that blend sharp intellect with atmospheric storytelling. Born in a quiet coastal town where fog rolled in like secrets, Ivy grew up with a fascination for hidden things—locked drawers, whispered rumors, and maps that didn't quite match the terrain.

Ivy remains famously private, rarely giving interviews and preferring to let her characters do the talking. When she's not writing, she's said to be hiking through storm-lashed moors, sketching story ideas on café napkins, or cataloging antique keys she insists will someday open something extraordinary.

THANK YOU.

Printed in Dunstable, United Kingdom